M000031084

JUSTIN "Q" YOUNG

DICKMITIZED

Point of No Return

An Erotic Story

By

Justin "Q" Young

JUSTIN "Q" YOUNG

Copyright © 2016 by Justin "Q" Young

This book is a work of fiction. Names, characters, businesses, organizations, places, events and incidents either are the product of the author's imagination or are used fictitiously. Any resemblance to actual persons, living or dead, events, or locales is entirely coincidental. All rights reserved, including the right to reproduce this book or portions thereof in any form whatsoever.

Published in the United States

For information about special discounts for bulk purchases or to book an event, please contact AccessJustinYoung@gmail.com.

In accordance with the U.S. Copyright Act of 1976, the scanning, uploading, and electronic sharing of any part of this book without the permission of the publisher constitute unlawful piracy and theft of the author's intellectual property. Please purchase only authorized electronic editions, and do not participate in or encourage electronic piracy of copyrighted materials. Thank you for your support of the author's rights.

Printed in the United States of America

Cover Design: By Firstborn Designs

DEDICATION

A simple hello can lead to a million opportunities. This is for you who took a chance on me, who saw a young man approach with a smile on his face and you took the time to listen.
Thank you…

PART 1

SWEETDICK87:
I just want to fuck plain and simple.

BIGBUTTDEEPDIMPLES:
Damn! You get right to the point don't you?

SWEETDICK87:
I mean…why should we act as if that isn't what the true agenda really is?

BIGBUTTDEEPDIMPLES:
Yeah, I guess you're right…

SWEETDICK87:
YOU GUESS???

I typed in all caps, showing my impatience. Already I was getting bored with her responses. What's the point of being on a website like FHLIRT if you just wanted to be cute? This was solely a hook-up site. I clicked off of that chat window on my phone and opened another.

SWEETDICK87:
What's up, what are you trying to get into?

I kept two pictures on standby for sites like this, a normal

1

headshot and a dick picture. Either I was going to pull you in with these dimples or the curve of my dick. I wasn't for any games. This was a regular for me, how I escaped the bullshit of dating or going through the motions. Forget what your favorite song was or what books you were interested in reading, I solely wanted to just find someone who would be willing to take the heat of this dick.

COOKIESNTATTS:
Waiting on you…I thought you forgot about me the other day…

A message came across my iPhone.

SWEETDICK87:
Where my pictures at that you supposed to send me?

Not even five seconds later her redbone, slender frame came across my screen from the chin down to her stomach. Her breasts were average sized with a few star tattoos placed across them. As I looked closer to make sure I was seeing what I was seeing, her nipples peeked out between her fingers seductively. After that picture another came through with her lying on her stomach, showing off her ass. It was small, round and connected with her thighs beautifully. You could tell she was petite, but undeniably sexy. Again, her tattoos caught my attention, this one in particular of a scorpion going up her side. The black ink contrasting with her skin immediately turned me on and made me sit up on the bed.

SWEETDICK87:
When are you going to stop faking and come fuck with a niguh?

COOKIESNTATTS:

DICKMITIZED

It's your turn…

She responded, but ignored my question. Without hesitation I sent her a dick pic. Part for shock value and the other to see what she would say.

COOKIESNTATTS:
You just made my mouth water…

Instantly she replied. I smiled. *Gotcha!* I thought. The next half an hour I continued scrolling other profiles while she and I exchanged messages.

COOKIESNTATTS:
You better be worth every inch that you sent.

SWEETDICK87:
The clock is ticking… When are you coming out to play?

I questioned while rubbing my dick through my boxer briefs. I was slowly getting aroused looking through the pictures of her and the other random scantily clad women I had saved. I didn't want to stroke myself, but I couldn't escape the feeling as I caressed my dickhead down to the shaft. Back and forth I went as I waited for her response.

COOKIESNTATTS:
I can be to you in about 35 minutes.

SWEETDICK87:
I'll be ready…

I replied as my dick jumped and throbbed on its own.

COOKIESNTATTS:
Text me your address to my cell because I am on my laptop

SWEETDICK87:
What's your number?

I typed, opening up the text messaging screen. She sent her number immediately. I was horny and hoping she was serious about coming over. I sent the text out with my address and paused for a second until I saw her response verifying she had received it. I then placed my phone on the charger, I climbed out of bed and went to the dresser, turned on *"No Love"* by, August Alsina, and headed to the shower. My mood was already set, but it was something about this song that just made me turn up that extra Virginia swag.

Taking a quick look in the mirror, I wondered if I should shave completely, but then decided against it because it was too cold outside to not have a little fur on. My chest and arms were void of any tattoos. I chose to always allow my face to be what attracted a woman, not some bad boy image she would associate with seeing multiple tattoos. My hazel eyes and light complexion always made women drool, but my dimples sealed the deal, not to mention the few piercings I had tucked away.

I grabbed my washcloth and stepped under the water. First impressions meant everything, so I lathered up underneath my arms and made sure my balls and pubic area were fresh and clean. After cleansing my entire body, I rinsed, exited out of the shower and walked over to the sink to brush my teeth.

When I returned back to my bedroom, I decided on a True Religion V-neck tee with some sweatpants. I stood in the middle of my room deciding if I wanted to wear boxers or not and quickly decided against it as I pulled my sweats upon my waist. I wanted her to see my dick print. I then proceeded to tidy up quickly before my guest arrived, but not before lighting the Tom Ford candle I had purchased a few weeks ago online from Signature Wicks. It wasn't that long after when I heard a knock on the door. I opened my nightstand drawer to make sure the condoms were there and then left to answer the door.

"What's up?" I said, smiling as I stepped back to allow her to enter.

Her full lips caught my eye because they were glossed up and looked inviting. Her natural hair was worn up in a big bun. I immediately wanted to just grab it and yank her to the floor to fuck right then and there but just stood there looking her up and down, with a look of desire in my eyes. She came dressed in a black, fitted baby tee shirt, leggings and on her feet were the newest Jordan's. Her petite frame was an absolute turn on. Her wrists were adorned with gold bangles that sounded off every time she made a move. She took a step forward and rubbed my chest as I allowed her to enter my home. What was crazy was I did not know her real name just her screen name of "COOKIESNTATTS".

"You have a little taste, I see," she spoke, breaking the silence.

"You want a drink or something?" I offered while walking into the kitchen.

"I want what you said you had to give me!" She replied as she followed me.

I got water from the refrigerator and took a huge gulp and placed the bottle on the table and grabbed her waist. A slight moan escaped her lips as I pressed myself onto her, forcing my tongue in her mouth. She raised her head up and I felt her body relax within my grasp as her hands caressed my back. My hands roamed, massaged and gripped her body from her lower back down to the bottom of her ass. Her breathing got heavier as she tilted her head back to let me kiss her neck and bite her softly on her earlobes.

"You feel so good to me right now," she said just above a whisper.

Before I could do what I had in mind, which was to lift her up on the counter, she put her hands on my chest and stopped. The kitchen was dark but I still could see her devilish grin as she dropped to her knees and pulled my sweatpants down. I began to spread my legs wider when I felt her grasp my dick and jerk me forward.

"Whoa!" I said softly. The feeling I got was uneasy and caught me by surprise.

"Oh wow, you have piercings down here," she said touching all three. I didn't bother answering; instead I grabbed the back of her head with one hand and grabbed my dick with the other. As if on cue, she opened and slowly took me into her mouth. She worked her tongue magically slurping and licking the undershaft, over and around my piercings, from the head, back down the base, while stroking my dick the entire time. Her slight moans were turning me on as I closed my eyes. My head began tilting back and I felt the urge to lift my leg up slightly. Her stroke game was like something from your favorite porn movie. She then gripped my dick with both hands and focused on sucking and licking just the tip of my dick. For her next trick, she switched up and started sucking on my balls.

"You like this?" she asked in a seductive tone.

"Yes, I do," I replied, as I looked down at her. She started slapping my dick against her tongue, ramming it in her mouth, and spitting on it when she pulled it back out. I could no longer hold onto the back of her head, because it felt like I was restricting her. I tried reaching down her ass to caress her pussy from behind with my fingers, but she immediately moved out of my reach. I laughed and tried again, it was like a game.

"Stop, I want to be in control right now!" she demanded.

"You are! Look at how you have me," I replied.

"If you keep on, I will stop," she responded with attitude.

I didn't know how serious she was, nor did I want to find out, so I eased up.

"This is my drug right here," she said while squatting down, putting my dick to her nose, rubbing it against her nostrils and sniffing it.

"Your ass is crazy girl! What the fuck are you doing?" I asked.

"I bet you have never had a woman put your dick to their nose before and sniff you like some drugs."

Now I was laughing because although I have had my fair share of females and they have done some strange things this was indeed a first for me. The sight of her on her knees and the serious look in her eyes turned me on even more. This scene right here was something made for TV.

"You have condoms?" she asked.

"Of course," I replied as I led her to my bedroom. Once in my room I went immediately to my nightstand and retrieved the Magnums. She then took the gold foil from my hands and tore it open. Her eyes never left mine until she reached down to take me back into her hands, rolling back the latex until it reached the base.

"Come here," I demanded, as I began removing her clothes. She stood as still as a model, lifting her arms when she had to and stepping out of the leggings to free herself totally. I could smell her sweet perfume. Observing her tattoos up close and personal while feeling the heat of her body, only excited me more. I then ran my hands up both of her thighs, reached around and cupped her ass, lifting her off the ground. She hugged my neck, laid her head on my shoulder and began kissing along my jawline. I gently laid her on my king size bed and pushed myself inside her. I knew she was aroused by how wet she was and how easy it was for me to enter her.

"You want to feel all of this dick, don't you?" I breathed in her ear.

"Yessss," she whined.

She wasn't heavy so I easily reposition her leg in midair. I wanted to get as deep as I could and I was able to go as deep as I wanted and like a trooper she took my entire dick inside of her.

"Mmmm…Mmmm…" She moaned while closing her eyes.

"I must got a little dick, this shit ain't nothing is it?" I began talking shit.

"Mmmm…" she responded, her face contorting.

I was pounding her harder and deeper with each stroke.

"Yeah, you might want to get a towel, because I get real wet," she suggested.

"No bullshit, I see!" That was the only response I could make. "Lay on your stomach!" I growled.

She looked for a second as if she might have noticed my change in demeanor and contemplated complying, but she turned over and raised her ass up in the air. I could smell her sex. It was all over me as I rubbed myself along her ass trying to get myself aroused again. I took my fingers and held them to my nose.

She turned slightly to look at me and said in a demanding tone, "I want to cum on this dick!"

With that, I positioned myself behind her, grabbed a handful of hair while jerking her head back and pushed myself back inside of her.

"YESSSSSS!!!" she cried out.

I pulled harder making her arch more as I got into rhythm. I watched myself enter and exit her, watching the juices from within her come out and build up along the base of my pubic hair. I hadn't realized it until I caught a look at myself in the mirror but my face was tensed, teeth clenched. I just wanted to beat the pussy up. She wasn't going to go back and tell her friends I had some slouch dick. We went at it for a while until I felt myself on the verge of exploding so I slowed down and yanked on my balls to kill the feeling. I pulled out for a second and began repositioning myself. This time when I entered her she did everything possible to slide up and away but I held her down at her shoulders.

"Baby!" she cried out.

I slid in easy working my way in and out. Her asshole was tight and I could tell initially she was uncomfortable but then the more I worked, the easier it became.

"Ooooooh...bae..." she moaned, meeting me stroke for stroke. She grabbed my hands and placed them on her breast and began squeezing them. Surprisingly she picked up the pace, throwing it back on me. The feeling was incredible, tight, yet wet at the same time.

"Take the condom off, I want to feel this dick," she begged.

As much as I wanted to oblige, I ignored her.

"Take it off!" She called out and moaned again.

Lord knows I wanted to feel her just as bad as she was crying out. When I felt myself on the verge of releasing, I pulled her tighter to me and pumped harder.

"This what you wanted, every inch, huh? Ahhhhhh!" I came hard. The feeling made my toes curl.

I collapsed on the bed and the both of us just lied there trying to catch our breath.

"You know, I don't even know your real name, only your screen name online," I admitted.

She laughed it off, but I could tell it was one of those things where she wanted to say more but didn't. I pointed to the bathroom so she could straighten herself up. When the door closed and I heard the water running, I hit the stop button on my phone from recording and started smiling at myself. The FHLIRT icon on my phone indicated I had several new messages and I couldn't help but to look.

CANDYAPPLE1983:
HORNY AF…U DOWN 2 PLAY?

She was wide open. A homeboy's baby mama I ran across, but didn't realize it until she was on her way to my house. She got everything she was looking for that night though, I quickly reminisced.

SWEETDICK87:
When?

I typed. It was still early enough for a second round.

Another message read: *"Lonely and curious"*, but I didn't have a chance to open that because I was expecting my guest to come out any moment. When she did, she was already dressed. *My kind of woman, especially one who knows when it's time to leave,* I thought.

"You straight?" I asked.

"Yeah boo, I'm good. You don't have to get up," she said as she collected the rest of her things.

As she headed towards the door, I stopped her. "Hey?" I waited until she turned to look at me. "Make sure you leave me a review."

"Most definitely, I will!" She blew a kiss and walked out.

I lied back in bed, stretched out for a moment before grabbing my phone.

CANDYAPPLE1983:
WYD?

Part 2

My phone vibrated as I turned the corner on Broad Street heading towards the Southside. Even though it was a little chilly outside, the downtown streets of Richmond stayed littered with students who attended Virginia Commonwealth University walking about busily to their destinations. I had downloaded D'Angelo's new album the night before and instantly loved the melodic rhythm of it so much so that it had been on repeat ever since. It was one of those mood albums that just made you feel a certain way. I grabbed my phone from between my legs in one fluid motion half expecting that it was an incoming text from Ashley. She and I had been going back and forth via text for the past hour or so.

I smiled when I saw her name and message flash across my iPhone. How crazy it was to be exchanging texts after reconnecting with each other after ten years?

About three weeks ago, I attended a family function in Virginia Beach where I ended up reaching out to an old friend hoping that I could get into something a little more stimulating than laughing, telling jokes and reminiscing about old times with family members. Keyonna, a girl from my old neighborhood, had rescued me from what was appearing to be a night of smiling, shaking my head in some form of agreement to stories I either didn't remember or was choosing to forget, or surfing the internet in between those conversations.

She picked me up and we went back to her place. Keyonna made drinks and I wondered how long before we could get naked. She had to have known the effect those tight jeans she was wearing would have on me. It wasn't so much her ensemble that got me, but the way her ass sat up and bounced when she walked is what had my dick on high alert. While I had one thing in mind, she clearly had another. With her glass of wine and her phone, all she kept reiterating as she stood in the kitchen was how good I was looking.

"I gotta show everybody how fine you are, Josiah. I've always loved your eyes."

I smiled at her excitement because we hadn't seen each other in over ten years. Sitting on my lap, we took picture after picture, and I hadn't realized that she had begun posting them onto her Facebook page until she started receiving comments and began reading off to me what her friends were saying. I admit, I loved the attention and as her phone began blowing up alerting her to new messages, I was willing to bet that their comments would be incentive enough to make her wanna ride this dick by the end of the night.

After about six glasses of wine though, she claimed that she was "trying to control her nervousness", we ended up in bed with our clothes on. I was restless as hell and attempted twice to put her hands on my hard dick. I even began playing with her nipples under her shirt, but nothing was reciprocated. I knew that I was done for when she started snoring lightly.

Later that next day I received a message from her:

Keyonna:
Don't think I didn't feel how hard ur penis was against me.

What the fuck? You didn't do anything with it, I thought to myself.

DICKMITIZED

Still feeling played, I didn't even bother to reply. When I signed into my Facebook account, the pictures Keyonna had tagged me in were also on my timeline so I could revisit and see all the comments that were made the night before.

One girl posted: *"Don't sit on the dick! Show it to us!"*

These women were off the chain! I thought.

I probably was wrong for doing it, but I sent her a friend request. New pussy is always good for exploration. I read several more posts before realizing who Keyonna was going back and forth with in conversation. Ashley Robinson. The Ashley from middle school, who I used to be so infatuated over. Immediately I sent her a request before seeing that I had one from her already. I accepted and sent her an instant message.

Me:

You should've came over to Keyonna's for drinks.

Ashley:

Don't I know it! I'm regretting it still. Send me your number though so we can talk!

And that's how it all started…

****

Ashley:

So when am I going 2 get my painting?

Her new message read.

Me:

I'm thinking Mon or Tues.

Most women who were attracted to me generally came at me the same; they inquired about or wanted a painting done after finding out how good of an artist I was. Then they would throw it out there if I could do a nude portrait, something that could be done tastefully for their bedroom, or if at some point, could they model for me while I painted. The sensual element and the connection you have while being in that moment painting, I tried to reserve for a select few. When Ashley started looking through my photo albums, she chose to show a little support by purchasing one of my earlier works.

Ashley:
Ok, good. I'm getting excited!

Me:
I like that U R excited…

Ashley:
Ever since I saw that pic you painted of that baby…OMG!

Me:
TY! U have me smiling right now.

Ashley:
That's the point! U R an amazing artist…

She quickly responded back along with sending me a picture of her laying on the bed sideways showing off part of her hair down her shoulders and the curves of her body.

Ashley:
I want something like this next time.

Me:
That's doable.

Ashley:
No other comments?

Me:
Nah, it would B inappropriate.

Ashley:
LOL...say what UR thinking...

In my head I was saying to myself, you know what I'm thinking sending something so suggestive.

Ashley:
So...

Me:
U R terrible...

I looked up quickly from my phone smiling, still driving but caught in the moment. I thought for a second the next steps I would be taking because she revealed earlier that she has been married for the past nine years. Ashley and Keyonna were tight and I knew they talked. But the way she was coming at me, I figured it was a case of *'the good lil housewife being lonely and needing a distraction'*. It was crazy that after all these years Ashley and Keyonna were still as competitive with each other as they were in middle school.

Ashley:
It comes natural for some reason, but I think that it's just U though. I have been reminiscing ever since Keyonna posted that pic of U.

Me:
Yeah she was turnt up the whole night.

Ashley:
I'm trying not to cross any boundaries but…reading that made me lightly jealous.

Me:
U have a husband, why would it?

Ashley:
Tell me about my pics I sent U…

Me:
All I could think about was how good UR lips looked and how I fantasized about them being on me.

I knew she avoided responding to the husband comment so I didn't press her. Just to keep things light, I played into the fantasy we were creating.

Ashley:
See U R not making this any easier for me. I'm having those same thoughts over here.

Me:
So we're on the same page after all these years, huh?

Ashley:

It's scary that we R. I want to meet up with U, but I don't know how that's gonna work with my hubby coming back N2 town.

Me:

We can play it by ear. TTYL

I responded while pulling up into a parking lot across the street from my destination. I put my phone in my pocket and proceeded to head into my favorite soul food restaurant, The Croaker Spot, where I was meeting up with a friend of mine.

The past couple of weeks had been hectic just trying to effectively manage my time. I was seeking gallery representation and wanted to put together a collection of new material, but at the moment things weren't clicking. Not that I had lost inspiration, just other endeavors were piquing my curiosity and time just so happened to be getting away from me.

As I opened the door I immediately was embraced by the ambience. The smell of the soulful dishes, the music playing lightly and the smiles on the faces of the patrons and employees alike, that was what this place was all about.

"Hey, Josiah," the hostess greeted me, walking up to me for a quick hug. I was a regular here and knew everybody. I returned her greeting and waved at a few of her co-workers.

"You want your usual?" she asked, walking me to my normal seating area.

"I think I'll start with a Long Island Ice Tea instead of the two piece dinner. I'm waiting on a friend," I explained.

"Sure thing, just let me know if anything changes," she said and went to greet other patrons.

As soon as I sat down my phone vibrated. It was Keyonna.

Keyonna:

That's real trifling what UR doing. U know that girl is married!

She caught me off guard, quickly changing my mood.

Me:
WTF are U talking about?

Keyonna:
Last night I was on the phone with Ashley for over 3 hours talking about U and how she feels she wants to step outside her marriage and have sex with U.

Shaking my head and thinking, *here we go.* I didn't understand why Ashley would involve Keyonna anyway.
Me:
What do U want me 2 say, she's grown.

Keyonna:
SHE'S FUCKIN' MARRIED!

Me:
So should she at least invite her husband then, make it a 3some?
I really was just talking shit now knowing it would piss her off.

Keyonna:
Don't play U know how she feels about U!

Me:
GTFOH! We were like 14 years old…

"Damn, bruh! Shit look real intense by the way you're hitting those buttons."

I looked up to see my friend, Steve, whom I had been waiting on. I placed the phone on the table to give my boy some dap and we began catching up on the latest.

"Man, you know how these women be on that extra shit sometimes," I explained.

"True," Steve agreed. "I see you finally have the website up."

"Yeah, it's a lil something I put together to catch all those who don't do the social media networks."

"Are you getting any new clientele from it? 'Cause I seen the paintings man and them shits look dope as hell."

"Here and there, you know how that is. But yo, let me tell you about this other site."

"Oh yeah?" he responded nonchalantly while turning to tell the waitress, who was now at the table, his drink order. I opened my phone, logged into my account and showed him some of the pictures and messages I had been receiving.

"Make sure you scroll this way. You fuck around and go the other way you might see something you don't wanna see, know what I mean."

"Man, you wild as a bitch! What dafuq the seven stars by your name mean? Like...you on some eBay shit?" Steve questioned.

I started laughing cause that's exactly how it was. "Man, you ain't gonna believe some of this shit if I told you," I began. I started off telling him about COOKIESNTATTS, and then explained that the stars represented women who endorsed me being "official". This was a straight hook up site, nothing more nothing less. Steve's face the whole time he listened while he looked through my phone was priceless.

"Y'all high yellow ass niguhs, I swear, catch all the breaks...I want in though!" He demanded holding up his glass of Jim Bean.

****

"Hey, I just wanted to hit you up because I had to shoot down here and support my cousin who graduates today," I began saying when I heard Ashley answer her phone.

"Awww! That's sweet of you. So what are your plans for later?" she inquired.

"Yeah, I didn't know what your schedule looked like so I wanted to know if seeing you was possible."

"I'm supposed to go with a co-worker to this thing at my job, but that shouldn't be long."

"With all that shit you been talking on the phone, you know I want to see you."

The past week we had been exchanging erotic texts and short video clips of us masturbating. Between her and FHLIRT, I was ready to be serviced. We spoke on the phone for another five minutes before agreeing to meet later. As I rounded the corner to Norfolk State University's campus, immediately the lines of cars slowed everything down as people were trying to park and get situated for the graduation ceremony. Flowers green and gold, balloons and other gifts could be seen in the hands of loved ones as they walked excitedly to their destination.

After I found decent parking, not too far from where I needed to be, I double checked to make sure I had my tickets. Lord knows I would've hated to get to the door and be embarrassed by not having them. Inside, a sea of people cheered and clapped throughout the ceremony which to my surprise didn't last long.

Before I knew it, I was back in my rental, hitting up MacArthur Mall in Norfolk since it was right up the street from the campus to get a quick graduation gift that I had totally forgot about. I thought about getting Ashley a gift just for the hell of it, but shook that off instantly.

How in the hell am I ready to give her a gift and she got a husband? Niguh, get it together! I thought, checking myself. I ended up catching back up with my cousin at the graduation dinner she had with a few of her closest friends and my aunt. Ashley and I periodically texted back and forth, I was trying to get her to go into the bathroom or wherever she was at to send me something erotic.

Me:
Just something real quick to keep me excited.

Randomly, I received a text from Keyonna inquiring if I was in town. I sat back in my chair and looked at the text for a moment before responding.

Me:
Yeah I am.

Keyonna:
Can U stop by my house?

Me:
4??

I did enough sitting and talking last time, I was thinking.

Keyonna:
I gotta have a reason to see U?

Me:
I'm with family right now and don't know how long this will be.

Keyonna:
I'm just having a glass of wine, but if it gets too late, I'll leave the back door unlocked so U can come in.

I reread the message again wondering if I was reading it right. This was wild. Two friends, two agendas, both on the same night, we might as well have a threesome. I shook my head. We'll see how the night plays out.

Me:

Aight

A half hour later Ashley was texting me saying that she was ready to meet up, so as anxious as I was, I excused myself from everyone and headed to the car. Making sure I was on point, I sprayed myself with Gucci Guilty around my neck and on my pubic area a few times. Looked in the mirror and then texted her again.

Me:

Let's meet out at the beach, that's cool?

Ashley:

Funny Bone in Towne Center?

Me:

Yeah, that's up the street so I'll be there in like 15 minutes.

It had been years since I saw this woman and here I was ready to relive my youth again. On the drive over I knew that if we were meeting then we definitely wasn't going to be just sitting in the parking lot reminiscing. We had done plenty of that over the phone. Traffic was light so I saw the illumination of downtown Virginia Beach within a matter of minutes easily.

My phone vibrated. I looked down to see on the face of my iPhone another message from Keyonna.

Keyonna:

Don't forget me tonight please...

I put my phone back in my lap, turned up the music and stepped harder on the gas. The Challenger jerked forward but held its own as I zig-zagged through traffic. By the time I reached the destination I saw that Ashley was already parked and in the corner. I pulled up next to her Lexus and we both smiled at the same time. Before I had cut my car off though, she was already at my door waiting for me to get out.

"Come here, I've missed you so much," she said extending her arms out for me to hug her. I flung the keys and shit back on the seat of the car and hugged her for what it felt like five minutes. She began sobbing and shaking in my embrace.

"Awww, bae, you're this happy to see me?" I asked.

"I'm sorry, I don't mean to be a big baby, but you are really here in my arms right now. It's overwhelming."

I pulled back to look at her in her eyes.

"It's all good, what do you want to do?"

"When are you going back to Richmond?" she asked with a devilish grin.

"In the morning, but I know you have a curfew tonight."

"Don't even go there. I know you're not hungry so what do you really wanna do?"

Looking at her I started smiling, lowered my eyes and bit down on my lip a little. "You know I'm always in the mood to play." I said putting emphasis on always.

"I really can't be long. Where's a dark place around here?" she asked while rubbing the front of my pants as if daring me.

"What about going to where we first met?"

She smiled and told me to ride with her. I grabbed a few things outta my rental, jumped into her Lexus, slid the seat back and watched her as she maneuvered the car through traffic talking at the same time about miscellaneous stuff. It didn't take long before we pulled into the school where we both attended. The only thing now was that it was so much different from when we attended, we both were in awe.

"They rebuilt the entire school," I said in disbelief. We drove around the front entrance area but the lighting in the parking lot for a late night was ridiculous. There wasn't a dark spot anywhere in sight.

"Head around back and let's see what's back there," I suggested.

It felt like we were staking out the place to rob it the way she crept along. Even back there it was lit up like a Christmas tree. I was getting a little frustrated seeing that we needed to head to another location, but quickly calmed down when she reached over and put her hands on my crotch and began massaging.

"I want so much to feel this right now."

"You ain't said nothing but a word," I replied. On cue I unzipped my pants to allow her to feel the warmth of my flesh.

"Mmmmm, we need to find somewhere fast cause I want to put this in my mouth."

At the stop sign she put her turn signal on and made a right onto Holland Road. Not even two seconds later she froze up and ushered me to zip my pants up.

"The police are behind us."

I looked in the side view mirror and sure enough Virginia Beach Police were following us.

"Head to that 7-Eleven at the light," I pointed. She put her signal on and began turning into the store parking lot. The police followed and when we parked, he turned on his flashing lights.

"This is some bullshit! Now he's probably running my information," she said nervously.

"It's aight cause you're Lily white. Imma go into the store and get a few things, throw him off." Ashley looked up at me as if I was trying to abandon her so I stayed put. The officer walked up and asked us what we were doing back on the school's property.

"Oh that was my fault officer, we both used to go to that school when we were little and being that I just came from outta town I just wanted to reminisce with her." It was a valid reason.

Taking his flash light out and inspecting the back seat area, he then asked us for identification. "We've been having a lot of people trying to steal copper and this late at night, I have to check out all suspicious activity."

I wanted to laugh just because of the simple fact of the way we were dressed. *Who steals copper in fuckin Givenchy clothes?* I thought. When he went back to his car I tried reassuring Ashley by taking her hand because she was looking unnerved. She turned towards me and leaned her head on my shoulder. It only took a moment for the officer to return. He apologized for the inconvenience, but reiterated that it was better to be safe than sorry. I ran into 7-Eleven and bought a pack of gum, some magnums and two drinks. When I got back into the car, Ashley was playing Drake's "Wutang Forever".

"It's yours… it's yours… it's yourssss…that's for sure…" The chorus went. I started nodding my head, gave her a choice between the Pepsi and the Ginger Ale.

"Where to now?" she asked.

"Try Mount Trashmore up the street. We gotta go through the neighborhood and then walk over."

Without questioning, she put the car in reverse and headed up the street. The neighborhood was quiet and dark so we found a place to park and sat looking at each other for a moment. Turning the channel on her radio to an R & B station and playing the music softly, she reached over and started running her fingers through the hairs on my chin.

"I'm so proud of the man you have become…" she started. "I remember when you use to be this bad ass little boy."

"We all need time to find our way, you know?" I leaned in and kissed her. Her small lips in comparison to mine felt engulfing, but she returned our passionate exchange move for move, even opening her mouth to let my tongue roam and play with her tongue. The more we kissed, the more her breathing intensified. I began rubbing her breast through the soft fabric of her shirt, paying attention to the nipples that were hardening. A slight moan escaped as I moved from her lips down to her neck. This was a girl who I had wanted so badly as a teenager. Tonight, I was fourteen-years-old all over again reliving my youth, but at the same time as a man, determined to give her the satisfaction she desired and needed.

"You wanna stay here or head on over on the hill?"

"I would love to walk up the hill and have you give me head as the cars and everything else pass by below."

"I can do that," she replied eagerly. "Let's go."

"Before we do though, come here and get on top of me. I want to kiss and love up on you."

Moving my seat back as far as it would go, she climbed over and tried straddling me as best as she could. There was no need for any exchanging of words. Our bodies knew just what to say to each other, knew how to communicate at this very moment. With one hand on my shoulder she took her other and swooped her hair to one side and leaned in closer to me. I reached up taking her face into both of my hands bringing our lips back to one another.

I inhaled this woman, her body on top of mine, the softness of her skin, the smell of her perfume, I took it all in. I loved to be in control but right now I contemplated allowing her to take the lead, just for this one day.

"You drive me crazy," Ashley whispered while grinding against me.

As hard as my dick was through these jeans, I knew there wasn't a question as to how crazy she was making me. The car was beginning to feel hot and confining, and her look right now was that of pure hunger.

"Come on. Let me give you this dick then."

"Okay."

We got ourselves together then headed to the trunk where she opened her travel bag up and pulled a towel out for us to lay on. We walked through the neighborhood over a little bridge leading us onto the park grounds holding hands the whole way. When we climbed to the top of the hill my phone starting going off and I half suspected it was Keyonna. Even if it wasn't, I didn't want to kill the mood with having a phone conversation so whoever it was I dismissed by silencing my phone through the jeans.

"Spread the towel out, right here, baby," she pointed.

I did, and then dropped the Levi's I was wearing down to my ankles, sat back on the towel and began stroking myself as she kneeled down between my legs on all fours. Reaching for my balls she wasted no time putting them in her mouth, lifting them up and licking my ass.

"Oh shit!" I said surprising myself.

I scooted back a little but without stopping, she continued by taking all of me in her mouth. She put my entire dick down her throat, began gagging but refused to stop. Each time she went down, she made sure she hit the base of my dick. The feeling was crazy and I couldn't help but to open my legs further apart. Now I understood why women wanted a man to go deeper cause every time she took all of me in her mouth I didn't want her to even come back up. She sucked on my piercings, running her tongue along the bars while jerking my dick in her hands.

"This dick tastes so good" she said before putting it back in her mouth. The next time she took it out she suggested that she lay on her back and wanted me to straddle her face.

"Fuck my mouth baby."

"That's what you want?" It was more of a comment than a

question as I rubbed the tip of my dick along her lips. She flicked her tongue in and out like a snake catching the tip and the underside. I positioned myself over top of her while she stuck one of her hands inside the waist of her panties. With her other hand she grabbed my ass and began showing me how fast was good for her while she fingered herself.

"Umphhh …mmmmph," she moaned and grunted, eating me up greedily. I didn't spare her one moment as I pumped my dick in her mouth as if it was her pussy. The closer I came to cumming, the quicker my strokes got. Sensing how close I was, she began sucking on me harder and jerking my dick.

"Ahhhhh! Shittttt!" I let out a yell, looking up to the sky. Ashley didn't stop as I know I filled her mouth up with my cum. Licking the tip of my dick and kissing on it gently, I knew she was nearing her climax because she started to slow up and get caught up in her own release.

"Oooooooowww… I'm about to cum, J, bae…" she moaned holding me in her hands. I watched her finger herself until I couldn't take it no more. I turned around and pulled both her pants and panties down to her ankles allowing her to open her legs wider. With my face directly overtop her shaved pussy. I bent down to put my tongue on her clit.

"Oh…My…God!" Ashley said slowly while grabbing my dick again to put it in her mouth 69-style. She started gyrating and pumping against my tongue the more I focused on her sweet spot.

"I can't take it, J!"

I ignored her pleas as I kissed and sucked on her clitoris while fingering her steadily. She tried to keep from making noises, but I knew I had her when her body began convulsing. I continued making sure I tasted all of her.

"Oh my god, you're about to have me doing some crazy shit."

"Why you saying that?" I asked getting up to face her.

"Giving me this dick like this, making me cum as hard as I just did. I don't get this too often," Ashley confessed.

I continued to run my fingers along her pussy, every so often stopping on her clit. Her reactions to when I inserted my fingers inside of her were the same every time, as if she could just melt. I kissed her nipples and the sides of her breasts, before returning to run my tongue back over the same spots. Every inch of me wanted to be in this woman. I could feel myself slowly getting hard again as she put her leg over top of mine, but then Ashley's ringtone from her phone made us pause as she scrambled to dig in her jeans and pull it out. She exhaled heavily and I just knew it was her husband calling to check in on her, question her whereabouts. But when she turned the face of the phone towards me and I saw Keyonna's name, immediately I wanted to say, 'what the fuck!?'

But instead I replied, "Don't tell me you're about to answer that."

"I have to, that's my girl."

When Ashley answered the phone, she put the conversation on speaker. Keyonna was talking in circles, which was an indicator that she had been drinking.

"You know Josiah is in town don't you?" Keyonna asked.

Ashley looked at me with her head cocked to the side, I shrugged my shoulders.

"Yeah girl I seen something like that on his Facebook page that he was in the 757."

"Do you plan on seeing him?"

"Key, I want to but I don't know."

"I thought y'all might've been together because he isn't answering his phone and I know y'all have been talking a lot lately."

"Oh yeah, nah his ass a trip though girl," Ashley said jokingly. I had already begun putting my clothes back on. I wanted to find out from Keyonna why all of a sudden she was blowing me up, but I wanted to do it outside of Ashley's presence. I didn't have any intentions on going to her house for real but now I was considering it.

As we headed back to the car Ashley sensed my frustration and tried to soothe me.

"I want to feel you inside of me, Josiah, but I don't want to rush it if that's okay?"

"I enjoyed what we just shared. Trust me Ash, I am not trippin."

"Thanks for giving me this moment with you Josiah. I hate to have to go, but I don't want my husband asking questions."

"It's cool, drop me back off at my car."

When she drove this time, she played John Legend's, "A Million". In the course of her driving I turned to look at her because I had felt her staring at me as she maneuvered through the streets. It was like she wanted to say something but instead was communicating it through the lyrics of his song. Reaching over she held her hand out for me to take hers and as our fingers enclosed within one another, she just smiled kissing my knuckles.

At my car, we hugged briefly before parting. I had several missed calls; three in particular came from Keyonna. I thought for a second to call but instead, I hit the highway towards her house. It had only taken about five minutes before I was pulling into her neighborhood off Laskins Road. Just like she said, her back door was unlocked so I proceeded to go in. The downstairs was lightly dimmed so I quickly found the steps and headed to her room. When I got to the top of the stairs and looked within Keyonna's room, she was dressed in a white laced negligée sitting Indian style watching, "No Good Deeds."

"Ohh, boy you scared the shit outta me!" Keyonna exclaimed. "Why didn't you call me to say you were on your way?"

"Because I didn't know for real if I was gonna come because the day has been long already, know what I mean."

I walked towards the bed, took my shoes off and sat back seeing the small trash bin with the wine bottle inside.

"You fucked her, didn't you?"

"Where in da fuck do you come up with this shit? Who you talking about now?"

"Now you're trying to play me, because I smell a woman's perfume on you."

"Keyonna, what's up, you called me over here, now you taking me through the bullshit?"

I leaned back down and started to put my shoes on, that was one thing I wasn't going to do, sit there and argue with a muthafucka. Behind me I heard her fumbling around on the bed huffing and puffing. It didn't matter though. When I stood to get up and looked, she had taken the negligee off and was grabbing at her breast.

"Josiah, why do you overlook me...am I not good enough?"

"Keyonna, are you really being serious right now? You fell asleep on me the last time I was here."

"You were supposed to take what you wanted if you wanted this pussy."

"Yeah, well, being that you weren't really coherent, they call that in most states rape."

Looking at Keyonna's thick body, there wasn't nothing wrong. She probably was a size 12-14, paper bag colored brown, with a couple small tattoos on her ankles and shoulders.

"Please go into my bathroom and use one of those rags under the sink and wash that perfume off you, it's driving me crazy."

"It's driving you crazy? Looking at that afro on your pussy is driving me crazy."

We both began laughing.

"Don't judge me, Josiah!"

She got up off the bed and stood in front of me. Staring in my eyes, she stood there for a couple seconds, close, almost body to body. She took my hand and rubbed it against her lips before opening her mouth to suck my finger. Our eyes never left from one another. With her other hand she guided me to her pussy. Her pubic hair was rough to the touch but as she slid my fingers within her, it felt like I was touching silk by how wet she was. I started biting down on my lip the more aroused I became. I couldn't deny or hide how this slow teasing was doing something to me.

Backing up she pulled me with her to the bed and sat down. Reaching for my belt she undid it and pulled both my pants and boxers down. My hardness leaped free and almost hit her forehead.

"I didn't know you had these piercings," she said while stroking my length.

"That's because ya ass passed out on me last time," I reiterated.

"Josiah, be nice, I've dealt with too much this past year."

She dropped her head and I thought she was about to give me some head but when she looked up again, she had tears coming down her face.

"Key, what's wrong?" I asked, sensing I got myself into way more than what I should.

"I know you don't want to, but make love to me please."

My thoughts were different, beyond making love. I had already done that tonight. This was about to be on some other type shit.

"Lay back," I instructed while kicking off my shoes and taking my clothes completely off. I grabbed the condom within my pocket and began putting it on when she grabbed my hand.

"You don't need it, I can't get pregnant."

"I feel better having it on though."

I climbed in bed on top of her and started kissing her full lips, moving to the sides of her face along her ear. She turned and I ran my tongue along her earlobe. Underneath me she began breathing heavily and grinding against me, while rubbing my lower back. I reached down, lifted one of her legs and rested it on my shoulder and positioned myself to enter her.

"Look at me," I demanded.

When she turned and opened her eyes, I bent down and sucked at her bottom lip while thrusting my dick inside. She let out a gasp but began throwing it back on me as I began picking up my rhythm.

"Remember, this is what you wanted," I warned.

PART 3

I feel like I could explode! Realizing how long it had been since I had a chance to really release. As I stood at the sink rinsing out the paint brushes I had been working with, I couldn't help but to get slightly aroused as my dick kept brushing up against the counter. It had been close to two weeks since I felt the warm, sensual insides of a woman, smelled the fragrance of her perfume or felt the softness of her touch.

Like a boxer who trains and abstains from having sex, I too, held myself to the same regime as a way to focus better on the paintings that I was commissioned to paint. The sweatpants I had on were thin and what I had usually worn when I painted because I didn't have to worry about messing them up. Right now, however, as weird as I was beginning to feel, I was happy to be finished with this commissioned piece. It was exhausting, but as I had put the finishing touches on it, I felt rewarded by its transformation and how it all had come together. It was a powerful expression of black love, two angels intertwined. The passionate embrace was reflective of what I needed in my life right now, as I thought more and more about sex.

I had FHLIRT on my mind as I came into the bedroom, powered on my laptop and anxiously input my login information. I sat down on my bed and could feel myself getting aroused at the thought of what I was on the prowl for now. There were several messages from a few regular women whom I always hit up, but *LITTLELOVEDOVE* is who I was prepared to video chat with right now. The green light beside her name indicated that she was online so I proceeded to message her to let her know I was on the verge of calling. The moment she answered and I saw her long braids cascade down her shoulders I reached within my sweats, grabbed my dick and began stroking it.

"Mmmmm... I would love to fill my mouth up with that juicy dick," she said, immediately she began fondling herself.

"I want you to let me be nasty and do terrible things to your face."

"Like?"

"I don't know. My dick is so hard right now that I'm looking at this pre-ejaculation as I stroke my shit and I'm wishing I could rub it against your lips."

"I can almost taste it. Then what do you want to do?"

"Tell you to get on all fours, grab you by your throat and fuck you in your ass one good time."

"Stroke it harder baby, let me see those balls," she requested as I tried repositioning the laptop closer. I found myself almost ready to cum watching her on the other end caressing her breast roughly and working the dildo at the same pace that I was going.

"Spread your legs a little wider, baby, I want to see that pretty pink pussy!" I demanded.

"Like this?"

"Yes, that pussy looks so good shaved. I want to close my eyes and imagine you, but I don't want to miss one second."

"I wish you were here to pull my hair and bite the back of my neck."

As turned on as I was, I had begun grabbing and pinching my chest. The sensations I felt as I stroked from tip to base were indescribable. This brown skinned woman had me wide opened watching as she held her knees to her chest, the dildo entering and exiting glistening with her juices.

"Ohhhh, I'm about to cum baby," she squealed.

"Yesssssss…"

My legs tightened and toes tensed up as I released and watched my milky semen spill over covering my hand. I slowed my stroke up but not before I made sure nothing was left. I grabbed the towel that lied next to me. I looked over at the screen and watched as she laid back on her bed bent over, but smiling back at me.

"You know it sucks that you're not in Richmond."

"I know," she whined and made a pouty face.

There was a brief silence for a moment, both of us probably wanting to say more, but we just left things where they were. After a brief conversation, we said our good-byes like normal. I closed the laptop and grabbed my phone to check the time, it was nearing 7:00 p.m. which meant that I needed to get myself together and head over to the ArtWorks Gallery for tonight's "Art 'n' Drink" exhibit. I sent out a group text to several people reminding them to come through and support, then made a post on my Facebook page.

The exhibit when I walked in was decorated nicely and had people already mingling with one another in front of the different art pieces. I honestly was impressed and excited as I greeted people on my way to my area. The DJ played light selections while visitors walked around talking and looking at the artwork that hung on display. I was being as assertive as possible, allowing visitors who stopped to get a chance to know me beyond the pictures that were hanging. I had just finished explaining how long I had been painting to this one lady when she cut me off.

"You have a nice piece," she said, taking a sip from her wine glass.

"Thank you, I painted this about a month ago and titled it 'Landin' to represent the serenity a child has in the hands of its parents."

"I wasn't talking about your painting," she responded looking from my eyes down to my crotch area where the Balenciaga Plissé denim jeans I wore fitted me to a tee. With a sly grin on her face, she took the promo card out of my hand that I was passing out with my contact information and tonight's features, but not before caressing slightly my fingertips, as she winked her eye at me then turned and walked away.

Cougars stay on the prowl, I thought to myself as I watched her ass sway from side to side.

"Hello, are you the artist?"

"I am."

I responded looking up from my iPhone to a beautiful plus-sized chocolate goddess dressed in crimson and cream.

"I see some areas where you can improve your highlights, but I've read your artist bio. I'm impressed that you have no schooling, just raw talent."

"Thank you."

"Do you know your art history by any chance? People like Henry Tanner, Salvator Dali, and Harvey Dinnerstein?" she questioned.

"I can't say that any of those names rings a bell to me, but I feel like they should."

She paused for a second like I had offended her. She pulled out a piece of stationery that held her sorority's lettering at the top and began scribbling name after name suggesting that I look these artists up. "I teach art at one of the high schools in the area," she added.

We continued talking for the next ten minutes or so before she moved on to look at the other pieces of artwork hanging up. I looked down at the paper she wrote on and folded it up in my pocket. I hadn't been with a plus-sized woman, but I was really contemplating putting that on my to-do list. Every woman that stopped or walked passed me caught my attention in some regard, either by the scent of her perfume or by how her body moved. I listened to the laughter as well as the conversations that exchanged between the guests just taking in this moment. Periodically, I made notes on my phone on things, but as time went on my thoughts trailed off planning who I would be doing afterward.

The video chat with *LITTLELOVEDOVE* earlier only teased my appetite. I wanted now to feel the wetness for her good pussy. Who better to reach out to than my Special K? That was my new nickname for Keyonna offline. Looking at the clock on my iPhone, I anticipated another half-hour before things began wrapping up. I looked around to see what the crowd looked like before taking a seat on a nearby couch. She was always throwing it out there that I could come through whenever so I pulled up her name and sent a quick message.

Me:

I want to see U so I just might take U up on that invite!

I knew that Keyonna wouldn't tell me anything except yes because of our sessions lately in front of the camera. She let me know her pussy longed to feel my dick again. They say women have intuition, but men have damn near the same and I knew she craved me just as much as I was craving her now. The tease was cute on the phone when we would video chat, but I knew when we finally came back face-to-face, I was definitely going to wear her pussy out no ifs, ands or buts about it.

Keyonna:

I was just thinking about U.

Me:

Oh yeah, what were U thinking?

I responded, wondering if we were on the same page.

Keyonna:
Just when I would be able to feel U inside of me again.

That was all the confirmation I needed. There were a lot of beautiful women in the room, some of which had begun departing with their dates as things began winding down. Like clockwork though, you had a couple thots who hung back hoping to get with an artist as they made conversation in attempt to be chosen. As much as I could've stayed and played, I needed to head in Keyonna's direction while it wasn't too late. It was funny how the turn of events happens from one day to the next. Especially considering it didn't take Keyonna long for her to get past the fact that I had been with Ashley, even though she didn't know what capacity.

By both women being so competitive though, having one up on Ashley I'm sure had motivated her to go passed her normal limits. I wasn't for certain what it was for me, other than our somewhat history we had with one another and the fact that I just felt comfortable with the idea of exploring her. By the time I wrapped things up and headed to the car, my phone started going off as comments were coming in from all the pictures I had posted from tonight's gallery event.

****

My cell phone rang and I looked at the screen and I saw his handsome face smiling back at me. There was something about Josiah that just turned me on.

"Hello," I answered.

"I'm outside."

I quickly got up from the couch and walked to the door, my pussy throbbed with excitement and anticipation ever since finding out he was on his way. I had played our meeting over in my head a dozen times, but this was different since he was actually here again. I opened the door and was greeted by his sparkling smile.

"Wow," I said as I opened the door wider for him to enter.

"Wow, what?"

"You are here." *And looking so good*, I thought

"What do you mean? I told you that I would come back, I just needed to get some other stuff squared away."

I closed and locked the door and proceeded to walk in the kitchen, with him right behind me following. I could feel his eyes on me for some reason more than ever and it was doing something to me.

"I don't know why I get like this when you are around," I admitted.

"Yeah, you act like I haven't been here before."

I led him to the dining room table and then took his coat from him to place it in the hallway closet. I liked his eyes on me and felt for some reason I was walking in circles. As I placed his coat on the rack, I smelled it and was immediately intoxicated by the aroma of the expensive cologne that lingered. I quickly snapped out of my daydream and returned back to the kitchen, where he sat at the table playing with his phone. He looked up at me and I did everything I could to keep from submitting so easily. Those eyes were piercing.

"So, ummm...how was the art thing?" I asked as I walked to the cabinet reaching for a glass.

"It was decent, I met a few contacts and I may have a commissioned piece to do, so tapping into new money is always good."

I opened the refrigerator door and grabbed the bottle of ginger ale off the shelf and walked over to the counter to pour a glass. As I looked into his eyes, I secretly wanted him to just take me right then and there.

"Would you like some?"

"Yeah, but you know what I really want," he flirted back.

I shook my head as I walked back over to the cabinet to reach for another glass. This dude here was something else. It had been every bit of ten years since we had dealt with each other, and as much as I knew he was trouble with that whole Ashley situation. I didn't care to think about it after our encounter that night. I knew I treaded on dangerous grounds, but I just needed a distraction from all the things that I was currently occupied with, so I readily welcomed what the premise was for his company tonight. What we had done earlier through our video chat only heightened my desire. I could not stop looking at his lips or his eyes.

I wanted to have sex, but not just anybody's sex. I wanted his. The thought of his scent on my sheets again would be just something else to replay repeatedly over and over again in my mind well after he left.

"Let's go to your room," he said, taking me out of my thoughts.

"Okay," I replied, feeling myself immediately getting wet.

I led him down the hallway and once in my room, he spoke again.

"So, where is my hug?"

"Oh, my bad."

I opened my arms to welcome him. I immediately just melted against his embrace. I did not want the embrace to end so I held on, closing my eyes, enjoying this man's intoxicating sexiness. I wanted to examine his whole facial structure, but did not want to come off like I was as awestruck as I was. He had this look in his eyes that said he was going to devour me and I suddenly felt weak in the knees. He walked me backwards towards my bed until I had no other choice but to fall on the bed. He climbed on top of me and began kissing my neck, then found his way to my lips. I took his tongue in mouth and began to wrestle with my own tongue as I made love to his mouth. He was such a great kisser.

I'm not going to lie…Josiah had me excited as he started to remove my pants. I wanted to stop him because I wanted to have some type of small talk beforehand, but I was frozen with fear. I feared that it would turn him off and this moment I wanted so desperately would end. I lied there in a trance watching as he removed my clothes, piece by piece. He moved with such determination as his hands began to explore my entire body, drawing circles with his finger on my inner thigh which then led him to my love box.

Josiah began to play with my clitoris as his kissing began to get intense. His fingers were moving in a circular, rhythmic fashion that began to arouse me and my kitten got even wetter with excitement. I moaned in between his kisses that alternated from my mouth to my shoulders that then led to my 38DD breasts. He paid particular attention to my nipples while playing with the areola with his tongue. My legs spread wider with each touch and lick. I wanted to feel him inside me and I think he knew that as well because he wasted no time grabbing a condom and then entering me.

Initially, his entrance slightly painful because he was bigger and wider than what I was accustomed to, but with each stroke my walls expanded to accommodate his girth. For every stroke, I received I returned the favor with wetness. I enjoyed all of Josiah. He moved my legs in every direction so that I could receive his fullness in my love box. He went as deep as he could and I did everything to match him stroke for stroke. Each time I climaxed, I squeezed on his magic wand, holding him hostage between my legs. We had begun to sweat with each long stroke. I saw that he was getting excited watching me cream on his manhood.

We sexed in a missionary position for thirty minutes before he repositioned me on my side, raising my legs up as high as they could go. Josiah dicked me down for what seemed like an eternity. I had to reach for my pillow and bite down to control myself from being so loud, moaning. My love box began to tremble each time he exited my hole with each stroke slippery than the last one. I looked down at him entering me and then back up at his face where he was biting down hard on his bottom lip. Between whimpering and panting heavily, I was heaving as he pulled on my braids and began whispering in my ear.

"Ooh, baby," I moaned.

"Oh, my God! You feel incredible…"

"Yessss! Give it to me daddy," I was lost in pleasure.

"Daddy, huh?"

Josiah felt amazing and he touched every spot within my sugar walls. He then turned me onto my stomach, putting me on all fours he entered me again from behind. He hit my spots all over again. I climaxed again from this position. My knees went weak forcing me to lie flat on my stomach and he took full advantage by going deeper and harder. The strokes got more intense and my breathing began to get tapered.

Unbeknownst to me, in a short time Josiah had learned my body and knew what spots to hit to ensure I received the most pleasure without denying himself. His breathing began to change which meant he was close to climaxing. I removed myself from the suction cup hold he had on my pussy. I took his manhood in my hands, pulling the latex glove off and placing his caramel, magic wand in my mouth, allowing him to feel how good my head game was.

I motioned for him to lie down as I carefully positioned myself between his legs and sucked on him long and hard. I played with his dick like it was my own personal lollipop. I licked up and down the shaft while playing games with his tip with my tongue. Each tickle made him move a certain way that let me know he was enjoying me as I was enjoying him being in my mouth. I wanted him to not only enjoy it, but also not be able to forget it either.

I released saliva onto his dick and made it my business to lick every drop off of him. I became mesmerized by my own sucking that I didn't even notice that he was about to explode. He did without warning and as he released the creamy surprise that coated my throat, I swallowed most of it and all of what I didn't catch, I rubbed on my face. I wanted him to see how turned on I was as I took his dick and rubbed it along my lips, kissing the tip.

"Damn, Keyonna!" Josiah exclaimed, breaking the silence.

"What? Is something wrong?" I asked concerned.

"Nah, that shit felt good as a bitch."

"Oh, yeah?"

"Yeah."

"Interesting that you would say that because it's not even my specialty boo!" I replied, winking at him as I walked to the bathroom.

****

I laid there in the mixture of our fluids for a moment getting myself together thinking about her comment. Her bed was a mess, disheveled and full of wet spots, but I laid back, legs spread wide open with my arm behind my head like a king who had just conquered. The bathroom door was cracked opened and I could see Keyonna moving around but didn't know exactly what she was doing until she returned with a warm washcloth and began cleaning me off.

"How do you feel?" she asked

"Like you were trying to prove something."

"Ha, is that right? I thought it was the other way around!"

"Nah, but you know I got to give you something to tell Ashley about because I know you want to throw it in her face at some point."

"No that'll be mean and that's my girl."

"And yet, you're fucking me knowing how she feels," I sat up shaking my head.

"That doesn't count because she's married," Keyonna responded with her hand on her hip and head cocked to the side. The look was priceless.

"Let's take a shower," I suggested.

I was already wanting round two. I just needed a moment to recoup. With Keyonna standing at the foot of the bed, her nakedness showing and breast sitting up, it didn't take much time before I felt myself hardening up.

"If that's what you want."

"Do you have any toys?"

"A small vibrator under my bed that I haven't used since...I don't know when."

As she turned and headed back towards the bathroom, I got up quickly. It wasn't until she was bent over adjusting the temperature for the water that I grabbed Keyonna by her braids and jerked her head back making her arch her back.

"Ahhhhh," she cried out.

"Remember what I said I wanted to do to you earlier?"

"Mmm...hmmm..."

We both stepped into the tub where the water was running at our feet. I pulled the lever up with my free hand turning on the shower while still holding onto Keyonna.

"Put your hands against the wall," I demanded.

Without missing a beat, Keyonna bent over slightly, placing both hands against the wall. The warm water felt good against my back as I adjusted myself. I had let go of her hair momentarily just so I could ease my way inside of her. Once the head of my dick made its way inside her tight ass, I pressed Keyonna against the shower wall. I was taking my time allowing her to adjust to my thickness. She cried out, reaching back trying to slow me from moving forward by putting her hand on my thigh, but I grabbed her by the back of her neck and whispered in her ear.

"No, I want you to take this dick."

Steadily she gave in allowing me to pick up the pace. I was so excited that I felt on the verge of ejaculation by how she felt to be inside of her this way, especially as she began moaning and gyrating against me. Reaching around to her clitoris, I began massaging it which made Keyonna instantly respond to my touch as she reached back and grabbed the back of my head. I leaned against the shower wall and lost myself in the feeling.

We continued exploring each other as we took a shower before both of us had no other choice but to tap out. I had lost the hardness that once stood erect. The more I tried to keep my head in the game, the more my body began having a mind of its own, so I conceded. We washed each other off before moving back to the bedroom. As both of us stood at the foot of the bed looking at the wet spots, we looked back at one another and could only shake our heads.

"This is all you," I joked.

"I'll change them tomorrow. I'm worn out," she admitted.

Throwing the towels that we had wrapped around us onto the bed to cover the wet spots, we both collapsed on the bed. I reached for my phone to check my messages. I silenced it earlier so I would not be interrupted or distracted.

My screen notifications read: *2 Missed Calls 1 Voicemail*

The automated voice recording read out a number that I didn't recognize. I let the voicemail play.

"This is Morgan, we spoke tonight at the exhibit, give me a call."

I closed out the screen, looking over at Keyonna who was looking back at me.

"What got into you tonight?"

"What do you mean?"

"The way you were grabbing and pulling on me. How you fucked me tonight was different."

"You know I introduced you to FHLIRT because on that site you see some of the things I'm into. It was a turn on to see you this morning on video chat. It was a turn on to have you dress up for me the other time. Role playing, tying you up…these are some of the things I want to experience with you. The way I handled you tonight is the way I like to have sex."

For a moment, Keyonna looked at me before sitting up and leaning her head on my chest.

"I never climaxed as hard as I did tonight with you, what's next?" she asked, winking before placing soft kisses from my abdomen all the way to my manhood and placed me inside of her mouth. I lied there in pure bliss enjoying her showing me, yet again, what her mouth do…

PART 4

"Hello," I answered my phone half asleep.

"I want to ask something of you. Can you talk?" she asked.

My eyes shot open when I recognized the voice on the other end and realized where I was sleeping. Immediately I looked over to my left to see Keyonna still sleeping peacefully. I watched for a second her breathing while looking at the screen on my iPhone to check the time. It read 5:26 a.m. I wanted to shake my head at this minor indiscretion, but instead, only yawned.

"Hold on."

In the background, I heard the slight noise of vibration which made me pause for a second. I tried to decipher if I really was hearing what I thought I was hearing. I sat up in bed, removed the sheets and then grabbed the towel that I had dropped to the floor earlier.

"You're wild right now. It's like 5:30 in the morning. What's up?" I questioned.

There was a pause for a second before she responded with a slight moan then whisper. "I've been thinking about you being inside me for weeks. I bought a toy that I'm using right now, and I just need to hear you talk to me so that I can cum."

"You know you aren't shit for going this long without contacting me right?" I responded, closing the bedroom door then walking towards Keyonna's kitchen in the dark using the light of the iPhone to guide me. Opening up the fridge, I grabbed the 2 liter cranberry ginger ale. I looked up at the cabinets thinking for a moment about whether or not to oblige her request. *Fuck it*, I thought. I twisted the top open and began drinking. Hearing the sounds of her pleasuring herself made me stop drinking altogether. She knew how much of a freak that I was and what could get my attention. I twisted the top back onto the bottle, sat it on the countertop and leaned against it before speaking.

"Are your eyes closed?"

"Mmmmm…yes," she moaned.

"Tell me what you're doing right now."

"I have my legs spread wide open and I'm massaging my clit with the toy."

"Hmmm, that's a start. If I was there though we wouldn't be doing it like that though."

"How would we be doing it?"

I came to the edge of the kitchen to look down the hall making sure the bedroom door was still closed. I exhaled, relieved that Keyonna was still asleep. I returned back to the same spot in the kitchen.

"Raise your legs up like if they were going on my shoulders then take the vibrator and slowly go in and out. Take it from the tip to the base, feel all of it."

"Yessssss!"

"Imagine the look on my face as I feel how good your wet pussy is, how it's turning me on and driving me crazy. Now look down at the vibrator and imagine that it's my hard, swollen dick filling you up. How I'm taking long deep strokes and whispering in your ear."

"What are you telling me baby?"

"You been running, but I got your ass now."

"Mmmm…Hmmmm…get me," she said seductively.

"Speed the stroke up, just like you know I would beat that

pussy."

On cue, I heard her shuffle the phone and she began moaning louder. I was getting aroused just listening as I leaned against the counter with one hand under the towel caressing the head of my dick, slightly jerking and rubbing it against my leg. It took only 10 to 15 seconds later before she let out a cry indicating she was climaxing. Now I was throbbing and ready to do the same.

"That felt so good, thank you."

"All you want to do is feel that plastic. You're not trying to feel this dick."

"Josiah, don't do that. I tell myself to keep my distance because I know that I'm married, but I end up fantasizing about you. That's why I called because I couldn't take it no more."

"Yeah, I hear you."

"My birthday is this weekend coming up, though. The girls and I are getting a room, getting some drinks and just hanging out."

"That should be interesting." A room full of drunk women can be scandalous I began thinking mischievously.

"I want to see you and sneak you back if you'll come."

"Sneak me back in the room, man shit, that toy is one thing. Muthafuckas gonna *know* I'm there if you get to jumping on this dick though," I responded to that invitation with assurance.

"You're just too damn cocky! I might just have to get us our own room then."

"Ashley, do you honestly believe that you're gonna be quiet about this dick - that you just had in your mouth the other week - once you feel this muthafucka? Get outta here."

"I said I was gonna get us our own room. I need to get loose one good time anyway."

"Be careful for what you ask for, muthafuckas known to go crazy after they get some good dick."

"I can say the same about this good pussy! Don't you be trying to change up on me."

"Girl, hit me up later when you know for sure about the room. I may swing by. I'm going back to bed."

We said our good-byes and I walked back down the hall to Keyonna's bedroom. *Of all the times to hear from Ashley, how crazy was it that she called in that manner?* I thought to myself. It had been a couple weeks since she and I had shared our intimate encounter, but not only that, I knew her and Keyonna talked every day.

As much as I had been fucking Keyonna lately, I knew she had been sharing some details to Ashley as to why she probably was fantasizing as much as she had been. I opened the bedroom door to see Keyonna had taken over half the bed by lying in the middle of it. I dropped the towel and climbed back in bed. The early morning sunrise was just enough light in the room, as I kissed the back of her calves and up her legs. She stirred awake letting out a slow soft moan but playing along just enough by opening her legs further apart to let me know to continue moving upwards.

Applying soft kisses, I stopped at her ass, grabbed her cheeks and opened them up using both my thumbs. I flicked my tongue along her hole while she tightened up and began moaning within the pillow she clutched. I was in a different zone right now and was trying yet again something different with her.

Keyonna rose up slightly and tried to look back at me momentarily, mouth partially open and eyes revealing a feeling of ecstasy, but collapsed back into the pillow as I plunged my tongue deep within her crevices. I continued to tease her and every so often, applying pressure to certain spots causing her to gasp and call out my name. Feeling like I had given her enough foreplay, I rose up, grabbed the condom, then positioned myself to enter her slowly. After listening to Ashley earlier in the kitchen and imagining her, I closed my eyes and pictured how it would be if she was here ass up and face down.

It didn't take long before I came and collapsed back onto the bed. We both just laid there for a moment, Keyonna rubbing my chest while I had my arm over my eyes.

"I am going to head home in a minute," I spoke.

"You want me to make you something to eat before you leave?" she asked, climbing out of bed.

"Nah, you don't have to do that."

When she returned and began washing my private areas with the warm soapy washcloth.

"You just know how to spoil me, huh?"

"Josiah, I'm not in any way delusional about what we have. When you're with me though, I will treat you like the king that you are."

She turned and went back into the bathroom where I could see she began cleaning herself up as well.

"You don't think I see them thirsty ass women hitting you up on your page?" she called out from the bathroom.

I could only laugh. I wasn't about to have this conversation about Facebook or FHLIRT for that matter, especially after telling her to stop commenting on every post I make. I grabbed my boxer briefs and pants and started getting dressed. The day had started off too good for the bullshit. Lately, Keyonna was saying with her words that our arrangement was cool, but the attitude and her actions were starting to show something entirely different. In my head I was starting to feel like falling back altogether.

"I have an order to knock out for the next couple days so I'll probably be tied up. I'm going to hit you up though," I said, putting my phone in my pocket and walking towards her for a hug.

Once I left, I made one stop at McDonalds before jumping on the highway. Traffic was minimal on I-64, so getting back to Richmond would be a breeze. I picked up my iPhone and sent my homeboy a message to meet me at the gym if he felt like working out. The way I was feeling right now, I couldn't explain it, but I wanted to do something besides paint.

****

"Josiah, you been catching the news, bruh?"

I looked over to where Steve was pointing. On the screen they were showing repeatedly an officer shooting yet another black unarmed man. This one was clearly running away from the cop and yet, eight shots were fired viciously.

"Man, that shit is crazy!" I couldn't say anything else shaking my head.

Standing in the gym mostly everyone, especially the black men, stopped and congregated in front of the television. There was no audio, but the visual was loud enough. From that video to the Baltimore rioting video, the reporter was saying that there had to be a better way to deal with these ongoing issues.

"Bruh, I can't even look at that shit anymore because it gets me too mad." Steve said walking off to another area. I followed him, a little dejected about how the more things change, the more they stay the same. I had been in the gym only about an hour and could feel my mood changing.

"Bruh, I do not have a life, all I do is work!" Steve said, heading towards the next station.

"That's how it is sometimes, man. You're not missing nothing though," I tried to reassure while finishing up my set of curls.

"You say that, but you stay telling me stories about this and that chick you done met."

Just as he was about to grab the 50-pound dumbbells and begin, he paused to get my attention, directing me to look in the mirror.

"Her name supposed to be something like Lena Love."

"Man, get the fuck outta here!"

"Nah, I'm serious. Bruh told me last week how he had tried to get at her and that's how she introduced herself."

Over by the squat rack, stood a white woman who you knew, was about her business by the attire she wore. Headband, armband with the iPod attached, spandex attire, water bottle and a focused determination that said, 'I'm here to work. Not bullshit.' She was curvaceous and very attractive.

"See, that's why muthafuckas be in here wearing cologne and not even sweating, they are trying to catch something new," Steve reiterated.

"I be trying tell these sisters out here that these white woman catching up." I joked. Looking at this white woman up and down, I couldn't help but to stop at the print of her sweatpants showing off her camel toe. That thing was fat.

"Man, I know you didn't tell no black woman that and didn't get cussed out."

A few guys walking passed, looked at me, looked back over at the woman beginning her squat routine, shook their heads and gave me the thumbs up as if they knew exactly what I was thinking.

"You still fucking with that site you had told me about a couple weeks ago at the Croaker Spot?" Steve inquired.

I frowned my face up for a minute, trying to recall the conversation.

"The joint with the broad's man that you was hooking up on."

"Oh yeah, I hit something up on that joint every now and then. Did you set up the profile like I told you?"

"Man, that shit wants me to give up my credit card information to respond to messages that women have sent me. Like, I got to be a certain level member or something."

"Yeah that's how it works. What, you thought this was some Facebook type shit? Man, you read the messages, they not playing no games."

"I know, but with accounts being hacked lately, I've been leery about giving out my info."

"True. Do that shit when we get back to my spot though."

The week took off more productive than I thought. A returning customer had ran across this idea that she wanted done on her living room wall, inquired if I would paint it and since it was simple enough and she was beautifully single, I figured what the hell. By the second day as I was wrapping up, Ashley texted and said that she would be calling me a little later.

****

"Did you have any plans tonight?" she asked

"Not really, I'm just in here making a few sketches for a new design I plan on doing on some shoes."

"I love how busy and creative you are."

"You got to be nowadays because people aren't as quick to turn over their money unless it's something that evokes an emotion outta them."

"So do you feel up to seeing me?"

"I don't even feel like driving right now to be honest, where are you?"

"Northern Virginia, I bought the room for us and everything."

"Already?"

"I wasn't expecting you to turn me down and I'm hoping now that this isn't the case."

I set the pencil down on the table and leaned back in the couch I was sitting on and stared outta the window. I really didn't feel like making any moves tonight.

"Who is all with you? I might get my homeboy to drive up there with me."

"My cousin, sister-in-law, Keyonna, and one girl from work that I'm cool with."

"Keyonna there?"

"Yeah, you know that's my bestie. Why wouldn't she be?"

I rubbed my face for a moment and shook my head.

"I couldn't pay for the room with my credit card because I didn't want to chance my husband looking at our bank statements so I had Keyonna get our room."

"Awww shit! That's classic. You told her I was coming up?"

"No, I just told her I wanted to get me some dick tonight and she was all hype thinking my husband was on his way up."

I stood up and walked to the bathroom and looked at myself in the mirror. *You ain't shit*, I thought with a smirk on my face.

"I can come get you and bring you back in the morning before we check out." Ashley pleaded making the deal even more enticing. I didn't say anything for a moment, still contemplating if I really felt up to an all-nighter.

"Fuck it. I'll text you the address."

"I'll tell the girls I'm going to Wal-Mart or something and leave out now."

I got in the shower and washed up quickly. I had shaved a couple days ago so I knew I was good on that end. Tonight I was thinking, was going to have to be memorable for as long as we had waited for this moment. When I got out of the shower, I dried my feet off on the towel on the floor, but intentionally let the rest of my body air dry. I walked over to the dresser and grabbed some clean boxer briefs, but no soon as I began planning the rest of my outfit, I decided against it. We weren't going anywhere but to the hotel suite, so it wasn't any point getting dressed up for real.

I picked up my phone and checked to see if any messages had come through while I was in the shower, turned on Big Sean's "Blessings", then walked to my closet to grab a pair of sweatpants. I decided on a wife beater and a hoodie. Back in the bathroom I applied lotion to myself while rapping some of the lyrics.

"I'm here for a good time, not a long time, you know I…waaaay up I feel blessed."

Even though I hadn't wanted to do anything, I was getting a little excited just knowing that in a few, I'd be deep inside Ashley.

On the dresser my phone started ringing. I was thinking it was Ashley letting me know how far she was, but it was Keyonna. I didn't even bother to answer. Instead, I called my best friend Steve to talk shit about the playoff games then called Ashley.

"Yo, how long does your GPS tell you before you arrive?"

"Let me see, umm, like twenty-three minutes, why?"

"You in a jet, ain't you?"

"No. I just know every minute counts and I don't have time to be wasting."

"I hear you. I'll see you in a few then."

I started up a game of Madden.

When she texted me saying she was outside, I walked out to greet her. "Don't you look good," I said as I opened my arms up to hug her.

"Thank you. Are you ready?"

"Mmmmm…you smell good, too. Yeah. I'll drive just set the GPS." I instructed. When we pulled off, she told me how she set the room up.

"I just want you to feel comfortable and make my body scream" she said rubbing my crotch.

"I definitely can do that."

"Ummm, sir, it don't feel like you have on any underwear."

"That's because I don't." I looked at her mischievously. On the way there, we mostly talked about things going on with family and work. A few times when I looked over at her talking she appeared stressed just about the condition of her marriage.

"I'm not going to complain, I just know we are two different people right now holding on because of our son. I have work and church, so I lose myself in that, but sometimes…we get weak," she trailed off looking out the window.

"You know we go way back, right?"

"Yes, we do."

"As your friend, I'm telling you we can go to this room and just turn up without adding anything sexual. Celebrate your birthday like two friends are supposed." I looked over and shrugged my shoulders.

Ashley leaned over, kissed me on the cheek and then caressed my earlobe with her hand.

"I appreciate that, but as a friend I need you to fuck me tonight like a whore you met in the street." Hearing her response made me bust out laughing.

"Oh yeah, I got you then."

The rest of the way our conversation was light and jovial. When we pulled into the parking lot she pulled out the room key and told me to go in first because the woman at the counter had been engaging in conversation with them the whole time and knew somebody that they knew back home. I got out of her Lexus and walked into the lobby of The Ritz-Carlton. At this hour there were a few patrons out and about, some socializing in the sitting area and others just figuring out what to do next I took it. I didn't break stride once locating the elevator. I opened the little envelope that my card-key was in detailing the room number and pushed the corresponding number on the elevator.

On the way up, I texted my homeboy Steve in case shit got ugly and needed him to come scoop me up. Although, I was for certain that this wouldn't be the case, I still wanted to cross my T's and dot all of my I's. When the elevator door opened I looked at the room numbers on the wall indicating which way to go and luckily, I only had to go a short distance. I slid the key in and entered, turning on the lights as I secured the door. *This is nice*, I thought, walking around and checking everything out. I stopped at the bed and fell on it to check out how soft it was. I didn't bother to move for a minute other than to kick my shoes off.

Moments later there was a knock on the door. I opened the door letting Ashley inside. I wasted no time letting the door close before picking her up and sitting her onto the countertop. We kissed and caressed one another until Ashley pushed away, feeling overwhelmed.

"I have to let the girls know that I'm back. They were blowing my phone up on the way here and I wasn't answering them until just now in the parking lot."

"How long will you be?"

"Keyonna ass won't let it go talking about she coming down here to investigate, but I'm going take a shower real quick."

I grabbed her back towards me and began kissing her again, palming her ass at the same time. The spandex she wore I knew would undoubtedly allow her to feel how hard my dick was, so I made it my business to position her crotch right on my leg. I caressed this woman's body with my hands and my mouth, tugging at her shirt for her to take it off. Her eyes were hooded with lust. When she removed her top and unhooked her bra, I went straight to her nipples, sucking and pulling.

"Ohhhhh, baby," she quietly called out.

We stood in the middle of the floor until I grabbed her hand and directed her to the bed.

"I need to go take a shower, J," she pleaded.

"You're okay. I don't want to wait any longer."

I laid her down on the bed, grabbed the waist of her spandex and pulled them down to her ankles where she then eased one leg out. I stood and untied the knot on my sweatpants allowing them to drop to my knees, climb on top of her and began kissing her neck, her earlobe and over to her lips.

"I've missed you," I told her as I grabbed her hand and wrapped it around my dick leading her to her pussy.

She hissed seductively. She rubbed me along her lips opening before easing me inside of her. I then grabbed her legs and lifted them up wanting to get as deep as I could get. We both were caught up in how good the sensation felt. As I started stroking, Ashley pulled me close to her, kissing me just about anywhere her lips could get to on my body.

"Bae, you know we didn't get any condoms?"

Damn! I forgot to grab the ones I had on my dresser, I thought. Even though that thought crossed my mind, I never slowed up my stroke. This pussy was too good.

"Fuck it, we here now," I began hitting it harder. Already within a short period, I could feel myself on the verge of climaxing so I pulled out. Ashley got up, grabbed my dick and shoved it in her mouth.

"Ahhh!" I exhaled, balling my face up and standing on my tip toes. She was doing both, sucking and pulling while moaning. Her head game was bananas.

"Oh, I'm about to cum Ashley...shit!"

She took my dick out of her mouth but kept jerking on it. Looking up at me she spit on the head and then put it back in her mouth. I couldn't take it any longer. I grabbed onto the back of her head and released.

"That was incredible," I sat down beside her on the bed and laid back.

"You know we're not finished yet, right?" she said getting up and grabbing a washcloth from the sink. In the other room her phone began ringing. I continued to lay back and watch her as she walked pass to answer. As expected, it was one of her girlfriends inquiring about why it was taking her so long just by the responses she was giving. She walked back over to the edge of the bed and rolled her eyes, whispering that she would be back in a little bit. I waved her off because I understood.

A knock on the door out the blue made both of us jump. My face was balled up wondering who the fuck is that knocking, while she looked just as surprise as I did. Without hesitating, I got up and put on my pants. Grabbing Ashley's arm before she walked off, I let her know

"Don't tell anybody I'm here."

Another knock came on the door.

Ashley looked confused for a moment, but agreed that she wouldn't. I went and stood within the bathroom with the lights out and waited.

"Hey girl, I should've known it was you."

I heard Ashley say.

"I should've know when you said that you were going to Wal-Mart, bitch, that you was up to something. Where he at?"

I knew that voice.

"What you talking about?" I heard Ashley reply.

"Bitch, I'm your best friend, you don't have to hide your side piece on me. Cause I know you didn't have me use my credit card on this room for your husband."

"Girl, let me tell you…"

The conversation between the two women kind of tapered off where I could no longer tell if they were in the room or not. I stepped out of the bathroom a little to get closer, but they had obviously left the room. In my head I was hoping that Ashley stuck to the script and didn't get in her feelings and start giving up information. The relationship between two good friends though, wasn't no telling what could happen. *I guess I will find out in a while if Key comes back,* I thought to myself. Just as I was about to go into the bedroom, my shoes caught my attention. I had kicked them off when Ashley came into the room, so if I was seeing them now I knew that Keyonna had to see them too. The wheels in my head began turning all kinds of shit even though I didn't owe her any kind of explanation.

"Fuck it, it is what it is," I said, falling onto the bed. I hadn't realized that I was extremely exhausted until I felt Ashley waking me up with kisses on my lips.

"Hey, sleepy head. What, you taking a power nap?" she asked.

"I called myself just laying here till you returned, but I must've closed my eyes. What time is it?"

"A little close to one in the morning."

"Damn, I thought you were showering and coming right back."

Taking her floral printed pajamas off, she climbed in bed and began rubbing on my chest and then down towards my stomach.

"I came as quick as I could get away under the circumstances. Mind you, my sister-in-law is upstairs and I definitely can't let her find out I'm nothing other than the good little wife."

"Hmmm, I guess you're right, you didn't tell Keyonna I was here with you did you?"

"You know she was really trying to get it outta me. When I started talking about the sex though, she forgot all about me not mentioning any name. You seemed strange earlier for some reason, are you okay?"

"Yeah, I'm good," I answered, pulling her legs onto mine.

She laid there beside me as if we were meant to be, playing with my face, rubbing my chest, to massaging my balls with her one hand.

"The whole time I was upstairs, I couldn't help but to think how I rather be down here with you, like this."

"Happy birthday, Ash," I kissed her on her forehead and pulled her tighter against me. For a moment we just laid together caressing each other. On the dresser the light from my phone flickered indicating an incoming call but I didn't even bother answering nor did Ashley notice. I lifted her chin up with my finger and kissed her softly on her lips, then parted them with my tongue. I made sure that she was laying comfortable as I caressed the side of her face, staring into her eyes.

Placing soft kisses from one side of her face to the other, Ashley began to respond by rubbing her sex against me. I could easily make love to this woman I thought but as I rose up and looked down at her, that wasn't what she said she wanted. I grabbed her hands and placed them above her head, spread her legs open with my knee and without warning, I entered her. She let out a sigh and I knew it was because I hadn't given her any real foreplay. The tightness felt good and it took about 3 good strokes before I really felt I was inside of her the way that I wanted. Underneath me she bucked back, trying to get her hands free but throwing her hips at the same time meeting me stroke for stroke.

"I like it when you fight back, give me that shit."

I grabbed her by the throat with one hand and then with the other lifted her leg up by my shoulder. I knew I was being rough, choking her within the pillow a few times because she pulled at my hand but I didn't let up. I wanted to let her know I was here. I looked down as I entered her and seen how she was creaming on my dick already, her juices glistening on me. This excited me more, watching how I felt to her. Each time I thrust in her, her breast jumped. I bent down catching one in my mouth. Her nipples were jet black and like little raisins. I sucked and tugged at them while Ashley had lost her mind in pleasure. She had me so turned on that I began sucking her fingers, and lightly biting her wrists. When I slowed down, it was only to tell her to turn over. I wanted to nut all on her ass and back when it was time.

****

Keyonna:
So U didn't see me calling U the other night?

I deleted it and opened up my email only to find several more messages from her. One held an attachment. I opened it and it was a screenshot of my shoes in the hotel. The caption read: "If we played Cinderella, would these fit." I laughed for a quick moment, really a chuckle, at how she was acting right now. I knew I had to call her, but right now I needed to respond to these new art inquiries.

For the better part of the morning, I was jumping from one thing to another and didn't realize it was as late as it was until Steve came by the house to use my computer. I continued to take pictures of my latest projects, cataloging them for future advertisements and promo. Looking at Steve, he was worse than me when I first made my account. All I heard was the pecking of the keys and some random dialogue he would be having with himself and the computer screen. I got my smartphone out and started recording his ass.

"Bruh, you good? You don't want anything to drink?"

"Nah, I'm straight. Josiah, man, I was supposed to been on this site back when you first told me about it. They are off the chain in this bitch."

"I tried to tell you," I replied, walking over to see the screen because I kept seeing pictures I knew I had seen before and faces.

"Hold the fuck up! You on my account."

"I mean, since you was already logged in I figured what the hell." I grabbed the keyboard and logged off.

"Nah, you mess around and see the wrong kind of picture on my shit making comments on previous posts."

"Bruh, you wild as a bitch," Steve said, walking towards the living room and turning on the PS4. Knowing I had been putting Keyonna off long enough, seeing her screen name right before I logged of reminded me that I needed to clear the air between us. I headed to the bathroom in my bedroom, closed the door and sat on the toilet. I scrolled to Keyonna's name and waited until she answered.

"Yes?"

"Damn, that's how you answer the phone?"

"Josiah, I don't have time to play games with you or for you to deal with me when you feel like you're ready."

"Key, I have been busy the last couple days."

"So you gonna act like you weren't just in that hotel suite with Ashley?"

"What are you talking about?"

"Oh, now you don't understand what I'm asking?" I exhaled deeply.

"So if you knew I was there, why even ask me?"

"You're a bitch ass niguh, Josiah, cause you don't even have the balls to admit it."

"What the fuck are you talking about? We aren't in a relationship. I don't owe you an explanation."

"Nah, bitch you don't, but when I sit here and have to listen to my friend pour her heart out about what she should do because now she feels like she can't look at her husband the same after what you two shared, that's the issue I have with you and these emotional games you're playing.

Aww man here we go, I thought.

I had told Ashley beforehand because I knew once you add the physical element into any relationship it was bound to happen for people to catch feelings.

"Ashley had problems and contemplated her next move about her marriage before I even came back into the picture."

"Josiah, I'm like not gonna be in this triangle with you and Ashley. I'm not gonna do it. You have shown me a lot of things and made me feel things I have never felt but to continue like this is damaging to my spirit."

"Alight then." I grabbed some toilet paper off the roll and began wiping.

"What does that mean?" Keyonna asked.

"It means I'm hanging up to finish taking a shit!"

Beep… beep… beep…beep…

I looked at the screen and it said call ended.

"Damn, she childish," I said out loud.

****

Almost two weeks had passed before I returned to the 757 area. It was one of those beautiful days where I had jumped in the car and got on the highway. The beach wasn't as crowded as I had expected. As I walked along the shore with my shoes in hand, planning out a few ideas, it dawned on me to swing by Keyonna's house since she was close. I don't know what it was, but I definitely missed the wild sexual episodes we shared.

On the way over, I started jamming to Fetty Wap's "Trap Queen." Even though the sun was beginning to go down, my mood was just upbeat. I knew when Keyonna opened the door she would still feel some type way about how things ended the last time we spoke, but I was certain that seeing me in person would change her disposition.

At the light a couple white girls crossed the street wearing no shoes on their feet, but I noticed that they were just as thick as any black woman I had seen. I made a mental note that the next time I go onto my FHLIRT account to start in-boxing a few just to get a feel for the way they think before pulling up on them in public.

When I turned onto Keyonna's street, the car parked in the driveway looked too familiar. As I approached her house and got out, I walked to the driver's side and looked inside. It definitely was

Steve's car. I looked up at the bedroom window and then back at my best friend's car like trying to process why he would be here. For a moment, I was stuck because I knew they had never met.

I called Steve's cell, but it automatically went to voicemail. I hung up and called Keyonna. Her phone rang three times before I noticed it had stopped. I looked at the screen of my iPhone to see if I was connected, I was but nobody said anything.

"Key?"

There was no response just the ruffling sounds of movements, and then there was laughter. She was laughing about something I couldn't make out. I looked back up at the window, but it was pointless because the curtains drawn. I could hear Steve in the background saying something, and then more ruffling sounds. I walked back to my car with my iPhone pressed hard against my ear. I couldn't hang up until I knew what was going on. This shit was driving me crazy that was my best friend. *I know he didn't just go behind my back like that,* I thought. Sitting in the car thinking about these two right now was starting to disgust me.

Moments later I heard Keyonna say, "It's yours baby." It came through clear as if she was talking into the phone. I couldn't take it any longer. I felt some type of way and jumped out of my car heading straight for her front door.

Bang! Bang! Bang! Bang! I pounded on the door.

"Keyonna! Yo, I know you in there!"

Bang! Bang! Bang! Bang! I pounded harder this time.

"KEYONNA!!!"

Her door swung open.

"What are you doing here, Josiah?" she yelled standing in the doorway with a robe half tied, hair all over her head.

"What the fuck you mean? What you call yourself doing?"

"Ummmm, the last time I checked, you were doing you and made it clear you was gonna be doing you."

"Where that niguh at?"

"Josiah, you are not about to disrespect my house with this childish ass bullshit."

"Steve!"

A minute later, the door was about to open wider but Keyonna had jerked it back.

"No!"

"That man don't need you to defend him."

"What's up, J?" Steve asked, looking clueless as hell.

"What the fuck you mean 'what's up', niguh?"

"Bruh, you wilding right now over a computer jank?" I stepped back and shook my head because now I understood when Steve was on my computer going through pictures and shit, that was how he found Keyonna…*LITTLELOVEDOVE.*

"Bro, this isn't no computer jank like…" I couldn't finish.

All I could hear in my head was them laughing when I called like they were really trying to play me. I rushed the doorway and tackled Steve. Keyonna started screaming and beating me on my back to stop but there was no turning back.

"Get off him, Josiah!" she squealed.

"You going behind my back, man!"

We hadn't thrown any punches. We were just roughing up each other. Steve was my best friend so I was hurt more than anything. While being shoved out of the house I tripped on something and fell backwards onto Keyonna's bushes.

"Chill, bruh! It wasn't like that and you know it. I met her on your page and we just got to talking."

I got up, wiped myself off and just looked at Keyonna. I didn't even bother to say anything. I turned and walked to my car.

"Josiah, you talk all that shit about how you be dicking these chicks down and how you got them wide open, but look at you. Shit don't feel good huh?"

I stopped at the driver's side door of my car and pulled out my iPhone. I opened up the text message window.

I'm pregnant... appeared on the screen and I was speechless.

PART 5

"Do you know how it feels to see the one person that you've had a crush on, kissing your mother? I mean like, really. When I walked into the house and seen the two of you, I wanted to die."

Looking up at Valencia and hearing her words made me realize how much of a drama queen she was. Her mannerisms almost made me laugh, but I knew that she was really serious. *This is about to be effortless*, I thought, seeing how emotional she was already.

I admit that I was anxious when I sent her a text asking if I could come by to see her. It was early in the day, but ever since we bumped into each other at B-Dubs a couple of nights ago, she was all that I could think about.

"Josiah, is that you?" a feminine voice called out from behind me as I tossed back a shot.

"The one and on -" I started to respond as I turned around, but was silenced by the sight of a familiar face.

"Valencia? Wow, it has been a long time." To say I was surprised would've been an understatement.

I didn't know what was up with these different women from my past, resurfacing all of sudden, but this one was different in a sense because she was my brother's age and not on my radar. What were the chances that on that night watching the national championship our paths would cross? We were both excited to see one another and catch up on life. I was amazed by how much of a woman she had developed into.

I pulled into her complex, snagged a parking spot closest to the building and knocked on her door. My mind was fully focused on where I hoped to take things this evening. This had a sexual element to it even without us having discussed anything sexual before my arrival. Maybe it was because all I saw were opportunities to fuck, or I was just that sexual. Maybe it was all in my head. Maybe it was something that I was hoping for when she responded by sending her address. I don't know. But, I was here now and I didn't come over to hear stories about back in the day.

As I sat on her living room sofa, I looked up for a second to see the hurt still apparent in Valencia's eyes, years later from when it all happened. I wanted to say something about her mother and me, offer an explanation, but I was now sitting on her couch and her mother had long moved on, got married and the whole nine.

Why dig up old shit? Why couldn't my presence right now be enough? I thought to myself.

Valencia's mentioning of her mother made me reminisce for a brief second about a time when Ms. Stephanie called herself giving me lessons on life.

"If you learn how to capture the emotions of a woman, you will have them at your feet. Get in their minds and pleasing them will be a simple task," she advised.

"Did you try to fuck my mama? Be honest, Josiah," Valencia questioned as she stood over me.

The intensity of her voice and the look in her eyes made me pause and think before speaking. After running to the ABC store to get some liquor and downing a few shots of Hennessy Black, I was beginning to feel the effects, but my judgment wasn't that off. I knew if I opened up and revealed the truth about what her mother and I shared, it would've hurt her more than I wanted to imagine. She crossed her arms and shifted her weight to one side of her leg, indicating that she was expecting an answer.

"Nah, me and your moms were just cool. She bought me a

birthday cake, which I remember to this day, when everyone else was too busy to remember."

I recalled a moment from long ago that still hung near and dear to me. Just thinking back on those memories caused me to reach for another drink. Valencia must have seen it in my actions, how endearing I felt that gift was to me because she eased up and sat beside me.

"That's how she is, always nurturing. But, that still doesn't explain why your lips were on hers. Just FYI." She placed her hands on my back and looked at me with her lips twisted. Her tone was no longer accusatory. She clearly was letting it go.

"I had three traumatic experiences in my life," she began.

"What happened if you don't mind me asking?"

She turned to look at me for a second without saying a word, contemplating if she should continue I assumed.

"You're trying to make me cry," she responded, taking another shot of Hennessy.

She jumped up off the couch and went into the kitchen. I followed her with my eyes as she opened up the refrigerator and pulled out a bottle of Moscato. I just reached down and poured another shot. She stood at the counter after filling her glass up, took a deep breath and looked up at the ceiling. I could tell whatever she was thinking about was weighing her down.

"I was raped when I was younger by a friend of my mothers. By her having to work so much at night, she didn't want to leave me in the house by myself. So, she dropped me off at her friend's house. He had a daughter around my age. This was someone that she trusted." Valencia paused.

I stood up and walked closer to the kitchen, caught off guard by the bombshell she had just dropped.

"One night, I was awakened by him getting in the bed with me naked. I didn't know what to do. I remember the night light in the corner kept flickering in and out. It was what I used to focus on while he put his hand over my mouth and rubbed his self on me. Ugh! It was so fucking disgusting." She shuddered in disgust as if she could presently feel his touch.

I reached over to console her, but she drew back slightly.

"You don't have to get into it. I was expecting something along the lines of a goldfish dying," I joked, trying to lighten the mood. "I'm sorry that I asked. I didn't know this happened to you."

As if she had not heard what I just said, she jumped into her other traumatic experience.

"The second traumatic experience, of course, was you and my mother. I had to deal with the feelings of liking someone so much and them not even knowing I existed in return. Which now, I understand. At sixteen, you wouldn't have taken me serious anyhow." She looked in my direction giving me the side eye.

I shrugged my shoulders because she was right. "And, what was the third experience?" I asked sarcastically.

"The third? Oh yeah, my third traumatic experience was this boy I use to deal with, gave me something that luckily was curable."

Wow! I thought. Luckily, she couldn't see my facial expression because for a moment I was shocked and at a loss for words.

Looking at Valencia now though, she was a woman in every sense of the word and held my attention. I couldn't take my eyes off of her. Wherever she would move, I was on it. She was a younger version of her mother down to the T! Skin complexion, mannerisms, and definitely sex appeal. Her ass was beautifully shaped just the right size and had the perfect bounce to it whenever she walked.

The form-fitting dress she wore stopped right above her knees, showing off her beautiful caramel legs. Every so often she would tug at it, bringing it back down from rising up her thighs. This was a woman now and not the girl I'd last seen years ago. Her insecurities or self-doubt showed, but my thoughts raced with carnal pleasures. I wanted her bad as fuck, and if my eyes conveyed anything at this moment, it was how lustful she was making me feel.

The two of us were something else, getting drunk this early in the afternoon. Our conversation flowed in spurts, not uncomfortably, but with purpose. Calculated almost by the way we both seemed to have ulterior motives. Although it had been awhile since we'd seen each other, a woman's behavior when she is contemplating a decision is almost always the same in regards to a man. Valencia's jumping up, going back and forth to the kitchen to down a drink said to me that she was trying to control her nervousness. I played along with it because I was horny as hell.

She walked over to the computer and tried to get her playlist going, searching she said to hear something other than the television. Her patience was thin, as iTunes was taking a while to load. After a few clicks and moving the mouse feverishly, she exhaled and shut the computer down before returning to her drink. I sat on the barstool looking her in her eyes.

"How old are you now?" she questioned.

I dismissed her question with a shake of my head and another sip off of the drink I held.

"I can figure it out, or call my mother if I have to."

"You wouldn't," I dared her.

Pacing back over to the couch, tugging on her dress she picked up her iPhone and proceeded to dial a number. My eyes were glued to her every move, as I caught a glimpse of her panties when she sat. I licked my lips.

"Hold up! Are you calling your mother?"

"I told you that I can find out." She signaled for me to be quiet. "Hello ma?"

I stood up, walked closer and leaned in so that I could listen in on their conversation. Being this close to her allowed me to get a good whiff of the fragrance that she was wearing. As I had my ear by her phone listening I looked down at her breast that were peeking out, I brushed my nose against her cheek almost grazing it with my lips. I was beyond aroused. My thoughts were racing, and I couldn't control the throbbing that I was now feeling in my pants.

"Remember when I told you that I saw Josiah and that he was looking good? Yeah. How old do you think he is now, ma?" Valencia moved away from me before I could hear her mother's response.

There must've been a series of answers that Ms. Stephanie wanted to know because Valencia began to get impatient.

"Ma! Ma, ma. Look, can you just answer me, please?"

I couldn't make out the response Ms. Stephanie had given, but Valencia started shaking her head like she had the answer to the million-dollar question as she began smiling.

"So you think he is like thirty-four now, okay."

She was wrong, but it didn't matter. I stood up and went back to the counter where I poured another shot. I didn't see Valencia when she walked over but felt her hands wrapping around my waist as she laid her head on my back and gave me a hug.

"You smell good," she said.

I slightly chuckled, "Oh yeah? Thanks. I've been thinking the same about you since I got here."

She came around and poured a drink, but just stood there staring off into the distance.

This girl ass is crazy, I thought, but it's always the crazy ones a muthafucka gets caught up with. A random thought popped into my head at that moment. I could hear in my head how people say men get in trouble thinking with their dicks. In this case, although the warning signs were there that she could be a problem, I was like fuck it.

Seeing her eyes tear up made me reach out to her and pull her to me. It was an automatic reaction for me to comfort a person when I knew they were hurting. In the seven years it had been since I had seen Valencia, she had endured a lot. I was certain that my sanity would be in question as well if it were me.

For a moment we stood in the kitchen, frozen until I stepped back and lifted her chin up to me so that I could put my lips on top of hers. It felt like she would pull away in that moment of hesitation, but I grabbed her face with both of my hands and began exploring her mouth with my tongue. Valencia reached up to me and put her arms around my shoulders and pressed her body into mine. As hard as my dick was through the jeans, I knew she could feel me against the soft fabric of her dress.

A small moan escaped from her lips as her breathing increased. Without thinking, I lifted her up and braced her against the wall of the kitchen. Her fingers caressed my head as she began getting more and more into it. I reached up under her dress searching with my fingers to find her spot. When I felt her pubic hairs, I quickly slipped two within the fabric of her thong and entered her wetness.

"Ooh," she breathed out heavily then returned to kissing me. I continued to finger her pussy until I couldn't take it anymore. I wanted to taste her. Pulling her from the wall, I laid Valencia on the kitchen floor. I lifted her dress above her waist, slid her thong to the side and began kissing her softly around her pussy.

I wanted to inhale her scent first and foremost before I put my tongue within her sweetness. When I looked up, Valencia's eyes were closed tight, and she was moving her head from side to side. I hadn't even begun pleasuring her, and it seemed she was getting closer to climaxing. Bending back down, I opened her lips and began flicking my tongue along her labia up to her clitoris. As I sucked and nibbled softly, Valencia gyrated and moaned while keeping my head in position.

"Mmmm…hmmmm…Yes," I groaned, seeing that it was feeling

good to her.

Flicking my tongue and fingering her at the same time was driving Valencia crazy. More than once, I stopped just to look at how pretty her pussy looked, and then would dive back in and suck on it more greedily than before.

I moaned as I tasted her. I wanted to feel this young pussy. I kept my face in place and used my hands to unloosen my belt. It was awkward trying to balance myself using my elbows to get my pants off, but I was eager to get inside this pussy. Once I got them to a point beyond my knees, getting them down to my ankles was easy.

I lifted Valencia's legs up in the air where I could see both, her pussy and asshole. Both looked appealing, glistening with her juices and my saliva mixed as I grabbed the head of my spear. I positioned myself, rested her calves on my shoulders and entered her with one fluid stroke.

Her pussy felt so good easing myself in as slowly as I did that I wished I had several more inches just to continue feeling what I did.

"Ahh!" Valencia yelped as she grabbed at the carpet, trying to ease back off of my dick.

"Nah, you aren't going nowhere," I whispered pulling her back closer to me. This was everything that I imagined it to be, warm, tight and wet. I continued to stroke her, getting into a rhythm until I had to slow down as I felt myself on the verge of climaxing.

I can't cum this fast, was all I thought as I pulled out.

"What's wrong?" she questioned looking alarmed.

"Nothing," I responded massaging her stomach and easing my face towards her pussy again.

"Oh my god, what are you doing to me?" she let out as my tongue tickled her opening.

This time, it was her asshole that I played with as I continued to rub her stomach, thighs, and legs. Valencia gyrated her hips only for a second before I stopped and entered her again. Although I went a little longer than before, the feeling of climaxing came back quicker than expected.

Fuck it, I thought and kept going knowing that once I got hard again, I would be going nonstop, giving her something to talk about.

My ass tensed up as I pumped harder. I felt the intensity of the sensation from the bottom of my legs move up and through my body as I slowed my stroke down and began feeling myself shrinking within her pussy walls. I pulled completely out.

"Why did you stop, Josiah?" She sounded alarmed while smacking the side of my shoulder with the palm of her hand. "Did you cum? You came in me, didn't you? Didn't you!" Valencia questioned angrily.

She pushed me off of her, got up and ran into the bathroom slamming the door. I sat on the floor of the living room looking like a three-year-old who just got scolded for something. Inside of the bathroom, I could hear Valencia cussing. I stood up and pulled up my pants. I knew I should've asked her ahead of time if she was on some birth control. When she walked back out into the living room, she had this look in her eyes as she approached me and stood face to face.

"Do you have anything I should know about? You didn't give me something did you?"

Her line of questioning I thought was unreasonable and I began to take offense.

"Come on, now. You got me fucked up! I am not even like that."

"Why did you do that then?" she questioned.

"I'm sorry, I just lost control for a moment," I reached out to grab her because she looked like she hated my guts at the moment.

"You could've let it go on me, on the carpet, something. Just not in me! Damn, Josiah, I do have a boyfriend."

She walked away. I followed her into the bedroom and continued to plead with her because her attitude was a little over the top.

"Yo, that's my fault, forgive me," I reiterated knowing I was tripping for not pulling out at least.

I started kissing her neck, softly and slowly. The floor was one thing, but now I wanted to take it to the bed. I picked her up and carried her into her room. As we fell onto the pillows that were spread across on her bed, I pulled her on top of me. She straddled my waist and started to undress me. It only took a moment before she was putting me inside of her, riding my dick as if she was a bull rider, bucking her hips forward and backward.

I wanted her to get loose and get fully naked. But, when I tried to lift her dress over her head so that I could suck and play with her breasts she wasn't going for it. Valencia smacked my hands away and repositioned herself. I palmed her ass using one of my fingers to massage her asshole as she bounced up and down and rocked back n forth.

"Shit...V!" I was on the verge of cumming again. This time, I let her know, and she allowed me to bust all over her. Thinking she was in a much better mood, I continued to lay there as she wiped herself off.

"I can't stay here. I've got to go."

Confused, I sat up and asked what was wrong. I didn't understand her behavior and the types of moves she was making so impulsively. She began mumbling something that I couldn't make out. I reached for the towel and wiped myself off.

"What's wrong with you and why are you tripping now?" I questioned.

"I am not supposed to be doing all this when I'm in a relationship. This man is going to be my children's father. I can't do this to him. I've got to tell him and hope that he forgives me."

I started to laugh, but caught myself.

"Hold on, what? Why would you tell him that you just had sex with me?"

I was lost. I knew that fucking her wasn't going to be a regular thing. Hell, this very well could be my last time seeing her. But you don't sabotage your relationship over a one-time fling, was the point I was trying to make.

"I have a conscience that won't allow me to be fake. What am I supposed to do if I pop up pregnant in a few weeks? How am I going to explain that?"

Though she had a point, if it were me, I would've just rolled the dice. Some things you just gotta chance.

She reached for her pocketbook on the dresser and walked towards the door, stopped then came back to the bedroom. She picked up her glasses, and I got up off the bed. As we entered the living room, a lot of things were going on in my head. I couldn't fathom the idea of going to tell your boyfriend that you just had sex with someone and expect that to blow over smoothly. *Where did they make dudes like that,* I thought.

I wasn't as drunk as I was when we first started having sex, but I still felt a brass of cockiness.

"One more time for the road," I threw out there, as I looked her up and down.

This girl was bringing something out of me that I didn't know I had in me. I felt myself getting aroused as I stood behind her, making sure she could feel the effect that she was having on me. She had one hand on the door knob and her back as she plead no. However, what she was saying out of her mouth didn't convey in her actions. I grabbed her by the wrists and turned her around.

"I've got to go," she whined.

I pulled her with me as I took a few steps backward reaching the couch, spun her around and grabbed her by the throat. She gasped.

"What are you doing? We've got to stop."

I was already unzipping my pants with one hand, with the intentions of lifting her dress up next. I bent her over then rolled the fabric up to her waist. I ran my fingers down her spine until I reached the crack of her ass, then squeezed her cheeks. She felt amazing. I began pooling saliva in my mouth, just enough to put on my two fingers. I didn't want to enter her dry, so I used the spit on the tip of my dick to make it a little easier. When I reached down in between her legs, she felt moist to the touch, but I couldn't tell if it was because she was already wet or if it was my spit that made her pussy feel slippery.

"You don't want me to stop for real do you?" I questioned, but not really looking for an answer.

She turned her head to the side and watched my facial expression, as I entered her. I looked down at her, licked my lips and eased the head of my dick inside. I slowly pushed my way into her sweet garden. Her facial expression was everything. She whined about wanting to leave, but her body told me to stay as she began throwing her ass back at me. In this moment, was a feeling every man chased and craved; the feeling of being inside a woman with good pussy.

I held onto her waist, slowing down for a second so that I could watch how wet her pussy was on my dick and how the cream built up. It was getting thicker with each stroke. Our bodies stayed in unison and for a moment, I was lost and wished she was mine. Valencia arched her back up and I reached around and grabbed one of her breasts, playing with her nipple through the fabric.

She didn't make any loud noises or moan as if I was killing it. Instead, she bit down on the sofa and buried her face inside of the cushions, letting me know that she was getting everything she wanted. I felt myself on the verge of climaxing and tried to hold off as long as I could, but this woman's pussy was a fantasy. I grabbed her face as I stood behind her and pulled her up to me. She opened her mouth, and I stuck my fingers inside, allowing her to suck on them while she grabbed at her breasts.

I began kissing and nibbling on her ears, caught in the same moment she was in. This was carnal, pure lust.

What if we belonged to each other? Is this how it would be? I thought.

Deep within my toes, I began getting that feeling that rose up my leg, making me pull and tug at her harder.

"I'm about to cum."

I kept going until I was at that point where I couldn't hold back anymore. I pulled my dick out and began jerking it to the same rhythm as if I were still deep inside of her.

"Ahhh, shit!" My semen shot on her back in little spurts, nothing in comparison to the feeling that engulfed my whole body.

Valencia rose up and went back into the bathroom. I was light headed but definitely on cloud nine. I had never tried to have as many orgasms as I did this evening with her. It was something about this woman that I knew I wanted to have again and again.

I pulled up my shorts keeping her juices still on me. *Fuck it, I can change when I get home,* I thought. It wasn't long before Valencia returned, grabbed her keys and stood looking at me as if I needed to do the same.

"I need to go. I can't stay here...I told you," she announced, looking sad in the face.

"Is it something that I did?" I questioned, looking like here we go again with the dramatics only this time she was pressed on really leaving.

"I just can't be doing something like this when I have a boyfriend. I need to be focusing on our relationship. I feel bad as hell right now. I don't cheat."

Seeing that she was serious, I didn't even offer a rebuttal. Fuck it, I had my fun. I looked around, double checked that I had my phone and keys, looked at her for a moment and walked outside to my car. Valencia wasn't too far behind me, getting into a two-door black Chrysler 200. I sat in my car for a moment and looked in her direction even though her windows were partially tinted. She looked to be on the phone talking, by the movements her hands were making. Valencia then pulled off which made me shake my head because even though she had grown up beautifully, something seemed to be still going on with her behind the scenes after all these years.

I started to text her, remind her that she would be sabotaging her relationship by admitting her infidelity, but realized at the end of the day that wasn't none of my business. So, I dropped my phone back in my lap and backed out of the parking spot. I thought about hitting the gym up because ole girl had me feeling energized like a muthafucka.

****

"Oh my god, what are you doing to me?" I recalled her saying while I had my face buried deep in between her legs. I knew by the way she was responding that she never had a man eat her pussy in the manner that I did. I didn't know what it was that came over me, but watching her walk around in her apartment made me want nothing more than to taste her. Just putting my dick in her wasn't going to be enough for me, I wanted the whole experience. Her pussy smelled so sweet. I raised my top lip to my nose to see if I could still catch a whiff as I closed my eyes to get the effect. Just then, my phone vibrated in my lap.

An incoming text message read across the screen: *Hey stranger, you don't know anybody now?*

I looked at the number, recognized the area code and knew it was Ashley. It had been about two weeks or more since we had last spoke in regards to her pregnancy. I hadn't responded because I didn't know how or what to say, really.

Me:
Nah who is this?

Ashley:
Seriously, it's your baby mama fool!

Me:
I don't have any of those because I shoot blanks.

Ashley:
Josiah, stop playing. Why are U avoiding me?

I looked at the phone for a moment then back at the highway. I hadn't dealt with either of the issues surrounding her or Keyonna since that day. Reading that Ashley was pregnant in the midst of finding out Keyonna and Steve were dealing with each other was crazy as hell. It was starting to look like some Jerry Springer type shit, something that I didn't want to involve myself in anymore. Knowing that I had to deal with the issue of her pregnancy at some point, I exited the text and pulled her number up.

"Hey," she answered.

"What's up?"

"I know you've been busy and all, but I thought I would've heard from you by now."

"I mean what do you want me to say, maybe this will help you and your marriage."

"Oh wow, you're going there?"

"What do you mean? It is your husband's baby, right?"

Ashley remained quiet for a while. I had to remove the phone from my ear just to make sure she was still on the call.

"Ash?"

"I want this baby to be yours."

I pulled up to my place and turned the car off. With the keys in my hand, I didn't know how to respond. No, I did know. I just didn't know the best way to censor my response.

"You've got to be kidding me, Ashley," I mustered up a censored response.

"I've been feeling the way I have about you, for a year, and it wasn't until recently that I have begun to be honest about it to myself."

"Girl, stop, get out of your feelings. You're fuckin' married Ashley."

"On paper, yes, but you have always been in my heart Josiah."

Putting the phone on speaker and sitting it on my dash, I took a deep breath while rubbing my face. This was some unbelievable shit that I had gotten myself into.

"Nah, I don't want that. I don't want you to break up your happy home just because we rekindled our childhood love for one another. No, that baby is your husband's and y'all are going to do what it takes to get your marriage on track."

"Our marriage is a charade. Trust me, you won't be breaking..."

"Ashley, listen to me. Fuck that, I don't have time for this right now."

"Josiah, you don't have to be mean. But there is a chance that I am carrying our baby. Women can get pregnant by pre-cum, too."

At that very moment, I wanted to hang up on her ass and delete her number solely because of her sarcastic tone. Instead, I remained calm and looked out into the city's street.

"Ash, you have some decisions to make, but that baby is your husband's."

"I guess time will tell, right? Talk to you later, J."

"Yeah, aight."

DICKMITIZED

Who the fuck wanted to go to the gym after all that? I walked into the house and sat on my king size bed. The day had been going okay until I decided to make that call. I reached over to the other side of the bed and grabbed my tablet. Without even logging on entirely, the notifications from FHLIRT were already awaiting me. I hadn't signed on in a few days. I wasn't looking for anything in particular, I just wanted to mentally lose myself in something else other than that bullshit ass call I just got off of with Ashley.

Immediately several messages popped up, invites as well. As I navigated through what I was going to open or save until later to read, one notification caught my attention and caused me to take a deep breath. *Here we go again,* I thought. I found it crazy as hell seeing how people alter their whole lifestyle to impress individuals they don't even know. Seeing Keyonna now focusing on getting her likes up with the pictures she was posting was both hilarious and disappointing in a way.

I had introduced her to this shit and all of a sudden now she had more confidence to flaunt. She was on here showing off her titties and shit. Reading her post and the comments below made me shake my head at the thought of what I'd created. Before me, you couldn't pay this chick to show you a hard nipple through the fabric of her shirt. Now, she was online calling herself *"MADAMEK"*.

I knew that I was responsible for Keyonna's transformation. I had given her that confidence that she so easily flaunted. Thoughts of her and Steve brought about another set of feelings. Without really thinking about it, one of Chris Brown's popular songs lyrics: *"these hoes ain't loyal"* came to mind. Although I knew on the flip side of things, she wasn't my woman, but I had given her the benefit of the doubt to have more class about herself than what she was showing.

After Ashley's call and now seeing this bullshit, I opened up the settings portion of FHLIRT, clicked the remove button and typed her name. This whole situation regarding the two of them was played out and I was ready to get over and beyond them. The tablet prompted me to confirm her removal and without hesitation, I clicked YES. As I was returning to my inbox, I received a new message alert.

It read: *"You coming out tomorrow or are you ducking us again? You know these ladies wanna see you up here in D.C."*

I went to look at the name of the sender then paused for a moment before responding. Cherie was an admin of one of the groups on FHLIRT that I was in called, Pandora's Box.

This was an *"invite only"* group where once you were invited in, you had 24 hours to post what you were 'working with'. You were given a WILD card to put with your picture that way others knew you were new. It also served as a discretionary warning if you were a male, for only females to view the post or if you were female, to have males only view. I had received one of my first stars from one of the members and since then, the other ladies had been flirting hard.

Looking at the e-flyer that Cherie had sent along with her message, there were two females from the neck down dressed in pajamas. Across the middle read: *"Patron & Pajama Party"* that listed the time and location. In smaller font also read: *"What Goes on Behind the Curtain, Stays Behind the Curtain. Pajamas Optional."*

Me:
That shit looks dope but to be honest, right now I don't even feel like the drive.

Cherie:
Well let me know, I can leave your name at the door.

Me:
Aight, I'll keep you posted.

DICKMITIZED

It was almost three in the afternoon, and all I wanted to do was take a shower and relax. Pulling off my jeans and boxer shorts, I was reminded of the sex I just had by the dried up residue around my pubic area. At the moment, that encounter seemed to be so far and out of reach with where my head and thoughts were now, it was as if it had never happened.

****

Walking into the shower stall, I found myself standing with my eyes closed and facing the wall while allowing the stream to massage my neck and back once I had adjusted everything so perfectly. It didn't take long to wash up afterwards because all I wanted was to close my eyes and sleep anyhow.

Upon getting out, I didn't bother to dry off. I simply wrapped the towel around me and walked over to my nightstand where my phone was and plugged it into the charger. Taking a quick glance, I checked to see if I had any messages before I lied down. I turned my ringer down, pushed a few things to the other side of the bed and crashed. The pillows felt amazingly cool against my face and within minutes I was asleep.

When I finally woke up, it was close to midnight. I couldn't believe that I had slept that long. I sat up on the edge of the bed, hungry as hell, but didn't know what I wanted to eat. I grabbed my smart phone and headed towards the kitchen. Without second guessing, I pulled out the container of milk, a bowl and walked over to the cabinet to grab the Frosted Flakes. If you asked me, this was a bachelor's favorite meal, cereal.

While sitting down eating I couldn't help but log onto Facebook to see what was going on. Being that I primarily used that page to promote and stay in contact with certain people, I didn't stay there long. Facebook was weak in comparison to FHLIRT. A few people within my network were online according to their names being highlighted with a green dot.

COOKIESNTATTS, CANDYAPPLE1983, KIWI804, RHIANNAWINFREY and a lot of the regulars were jumping from chat to chat. In one chat room someone had posted the question: "What is good pussy?"

A few of the ladies were making comments, but I hadn't seen anything coming from a male yet. I took another spoonful of the cereal, thought about it for a second and then added my response.

I posted:

Good pussy in my opinion is about the overall experience a man has with a woman. All pussies get wet. Some wetter than others, some pussies move better than others, but if that woman can create an experience, that man will walk away feeling like the king of the jungle.

Lady #1 responded:

So you're saying it just being wet isn't good enough?

Lady #2 asked:

What do you mean 'create an experience'?

The questions were starting to come in now that they saw a male was present in this chat.

I gladly elaborated:

Honestly, I've had a lady use lube on several occasions and called herself getting the toys out, and I still feel like she was mediocre. I also have only kissed a woman, ate her pussy and brought her to an orgasm and been in tuned with her just as much as a woman I was fucking. It's the mental connection.

I then flipped a question right back on these ladies.

Me:

DICKMITIZED

So tell me what you want?

Lady #3 responded:
I want him to indulge in my every curve and feast on my ever desire.

Lady #4 chimed in:
I want him to sex me as if his very existence depended on it."

Both responses came almost simultaneously.

I started to chuckle at their checklist because they obviously forgot where they were, in a FHLIRT chat room.
I responded:
Damn y'all aren't tryna have just sex n' chill, you tryna make a muthafucka go to Jared and get a ring.

Lady #3 snapped:
You asked me what I wanted…now you sound as if I'm Alice in Wonderland.

I reality checked Lady #3:
Nah I wouldn't say that but the type of passion you're looking for, you're not gonna find that within this group, nor online, but I may be wrong.

Lady #1 asked:
So good men don't get online?

I sighed as I responded:
Of course, but look at the type of site we are on. How many times has a dude IM'ed you his dick without you asking to see it?

Lady #1 agreed:

True...

I responded:
See that's the type of group we're in. People just wanna live in the moment.

   Lady #4 asked:
Who says that I'm looking for what I described within this group? Everything has a purpose, correct?

For the next fifteen minutes, I was in and out of chat rooms, scrolling through pictures and on some late night lurking shit. With the night being over and too late to expect someone to come by, I headed back to my room to get in bed.

****

I woke up in the morning to the sound of raindrops beating against the windows. It was melodic in a sense that I was inclined to roll over and go back to sleep. However, I had scheduled a 10:30 a.m. appointment at my studio to show a potential client my latest series of paintings and it was already after nine. Reluctantly I sat up, stretched and yawned one good time before placing my feet on the floor. I whispered a quick prayer of thanks, grabbed my iPhone and headed to the bathroom to make a quick dump.

   It was Friday, and I needed to secure some sales because I didn't have the traditional job that paid every week or the security of just having to clock in and receive a paycheck. My life was a little more stressful than that because I lived off the sales of my paintings. Sometimes, I had the luxury of setting up appointments and if not I'd sell original pieces or prints. This new buyer was a husband and wife couple who moved into the area and was looking for Black Art pieces to adorn their residence. Looking for email correspondences,

I quickly responded then jumped into the shower.

By the time I got out and reached my destination, I had time to cut the lights on and walk back into my office before the couple called saying that they were pulling up. I figured this appointment would be quick because I'd just rented this space and only had a few pieces hanging up on display. I wanted to have refreshments to offer, so I rushed to put a few things out on the counter.

"Good Morning, I'm David, and this is my wife, Tangie," the husband announced, greeting me with a firm handshake as his wife smiled and then did the same.

"Good morning. As you know my name is Josiah, welcome to my studio."

"My wife and I were eating at The Croaker Spot and her sorority sister suggested that we look you up to do some work for us."

"Oh yeah, that's one of my favorite spots to eat. I love that place. Are you looking for something in particular?"

"Well, as I mentioned in the email, we just moved in over at Rocketts Landing and the view over there is amazing by the water," David began his spiel with enthusiasm.

"Yes, indeed it is," I agreed.

"As far as something in particular, we would like to see what you have already that we may purchase," Tangie interjected. "As well as possibly having you do a commissioned piece to bring a little life into the place."

Hearing those words made my day because it said to me that they came out to spend some money. I took them to my studio showing them the layout of things and discussed with them how I came to do what I love. I had a portfolio that I pulled out and allowed them to flip through it to see past work. I then walked them around to where I had some of my paintings hung up on the wall. Although the space was wide open and they could see everything from the door, I wanted them to be able to have a closer look at things.

While showing them, "Runaway Love" one of the paintings I'd been working, I began to explain how it was inspired by the fleeting feeling one has when they think what is theirs, truly isn't. I then got into color theory, explaining the usage of why I chose the bold colors that I did to capture the essence of the woman depicted in my painting.

This was a different kind of painting for me, one that I had started weeks earlier after the incident regarding Keyonna.

"You have a way of expressing emotion through your paintings. This is phenomenal," Tangie responded.

"You have an amazing gift. Give us a moment, Josiah." David pulled his wife to the side and began speaking with her. It wasn't long before they got my attention and presented me with a three thousand dollar check.

"My wife and I started collecting black art a few years ago and had acquired about six pieces that we are fond of. We see greatness in you, and we want to invest that's why I wrote such a large check. Whatever is left from the sale, we want to have that put towards a commissioned piece if that's okay."

Ecstatic that this was happening so easily, I couldn't do anything other than thanking them both. We took a selfie in front of their new painting, and I posted it on my Facebook business page. After getting their shipping information, I walked them to their car, thanked them again and went back to the studio to finish up the rest of the paperwork.

My iPhone vibrated as an incoming text flashed across the screen: *I think we should talk.*

It was from Keyonna. Now all of a sudden she wanted to reach out to me. I picked up the phone that I had at the studio, dismissed the text and tried calling Valencia. It rang a couple of times and then went to voicemail. Thinking she probably was the type that didn't answer unknown numbers, I texted from my smart phone.

Me:

U know I've been thinking about U right?

It was true.

Valencia:

This is starting to feel weird.

Me:

UR overthinking this

I texted back, shaking my head about how she wanted to come clean about what we did to her boyfriend. I waited a couple of minutes, looking at my phone periodically, but didn't see any indication that she was responding back. I was becoming impatient, so I sent her another text.

Me:

WYD? lemme come over and see U

Valencia:

Watching a movie…and are U kidding me?

Her response was priceless. I could see her facial expressions as if she was sitting in front of me. She was very theatrical.

Valencia:

Considering what happened last time that might not be a good idea.

Me:

But it wasn't bad, come on, you're starting to make me feel like you regret what we shared.

It was true. I was beginning to feel rejected, something that never happened to me after a sexual encounter. If anything, I was the one ducking and dodging the woman. As I sat looking at the screen waiting for a response, I was becoming more and more frustrated. Valencia was playing games.

A new text message read: *Patron & Pajama Party Tonight!!*

It was a reminder from Cherie.

Fuck this, I'm going to celebrate tonight, I thought. I called my homeboy Steve because at the end of the day, he was like a brother to me and I couldn't let pussy get in the way of that. He had been navigating through FHLIRT pretty good on his own, so it only made sense for him to go with me to the meet and greet.

It didn't take long to shoot up to D.C. and get into the swing of things. Marijuana was legal now, so it seemed like everybody was high as hell at the spot by the time we arrived. After we parked and got settled, we both fell into the mix of meeting some of the members from Pandora's Box that we'd only had the opportunity to talk to online.

I played the bar real close keeping my eye on Katrina, better known as KitKat. We sent each other messages now and then, flirted and sent each other pictures, but never before did I have the opportunity to be face to face with her. Our conversation was fluid. We laughed and pointed out members in the group who needed to sit down because even though we had some young members, we had ones that refused to call it quits too.

I turned lock eyes with her, and then responded, "You are trouble."

"I know," she said, rubbing my back. For a moment we both just shook our heads at one another.

"Let's take another shot," she suggested, ordering a round of 1800.

"What up, J? It's good to see that you finally made it out," a passerby spoke as he raised his Heineken in the air. I just nodded and got back into my conversation with Katrina.

"Go to the bathroom," I whispered in her ear. We had been laughing and making small talk thus far about trivial things. Nothing of real importance, just the basic maneuvering a man and woman did with one another in the process of feeling each other out. Her facial expressions changed momentarily, caught off guard and trying to register what I was proposing. We were just laughing at a funny post someone had made on FHLIRT, and now she turned to look at how serious I was being. I reached down to rub her lower back as she had done me moments earlier while raising my eyebrow up a little.

There's nothing like being in the moment, I thought as I took another sip of the Grand Marnier 100 I was already drinking on. The room was electrified with personalities, mostly mixed with Pandora's Box members and regularly invited guest. I realized that Katrina seemed more comfortable behind the computer than in person, but I had to put her to the test. She looked around at the other individuals who were close. They all looked to be deeply involved in their conversations to even pay attention to what we were contemplating.

I looked as well, smiling at those whose eyes I made contact with. My thoughts were preoccupied on what I was about to do to this woman versus wondering if they would miss me once they realized I had snuck off.

Turning to look back at her, I leaned in again, "Do you need an incentive?" I pressed my crotch against her hand that was on her knee.

I was already aroused, turned on mostly by watching her and imagining her mouth around the rim of my dick. I knew from posts she made online within our secret group that she loved to suck some dick. I loved how she felt, rubbing my hands along her thighs, excited with anticipation of what could happen next. Katrina was curvaceous, sexy and with rich, dark chocolate skin. The attitude and confidence she exuded would rival against the best smaller sized woman; you couldn't tell her anything. She showed her flexibility and sexiness in the pictures that she posted online. Now, she was finally in front of me, I wanted to put that shit to the test.

"Oh, you think you're going to get it that quick, huh?" she responded.

"Whether now or later, you know you want to fuck with me."

"See, that's the problem right there, you have all of these bitches catering to you and gassing your head up."

"And…you're holding out, why? To prove that you're not thirsty? How old are we again?" I shook my head. Our conversation was entertaining and sexual, yet calculating. A few minutes later, she looked at me for a moment, grabbed her shot of 1800 and swallowed the last of its contents.

"You better be right behind me."

I'm down on your ass, I thought as we both snaked our way towards the bathroom. As she approached the door, she opened it and went in without looking back. I had been maybe two steps behind her so as the door was slowly on the verge of closing I was able to reach out and catch the handle. On the wall there was a sign that clearly indicated Women, but of course, that was ignored as I closed the door behind me. Katrina stood at the sink with her fist at her mouth, biting down on her finger as I came in. I didn't get a chance to do anything before she rushed towards me putting her arms around my neck. She pressed her body against mine and put her lips on mine.

It appeared she was playing the role right along with me as we kissed one another while her hands were trying to unbuckle my pants.

"Damn, Josiah, who the fuck wears button fly jeans?"

She was scrambling trying to unfasten them, so I stopped her and did it myself. She knelt down and caught my dick as soon as it jumped free from my boxer briefs. Instantly, she grabbed the head of my penis and ran her tongue around it before taking the entire thing into her mouth.

"Oh shit," I wasn't ready for what that felt like as I put my hand against the wall.

She slurped and sucked, and as I was about to close my eyes someone busted through the door. Katrina jumped back, but it wasn't too far she could go. The person coming into the bathroom looked both of us in our faces, seen what we were in the midst of doing and apologized closing the door.

"Shit, you didn't lock the door?" she accused.

I thought I did, but Katrina had rushed me so fast that I couldn't be for certain.

She stood up and went to the sink. Turning the water on, she began rinsing her mouth out. There was a slight knock on the door. I cracked it open and saw the shirt of an employee.

"Sir, you know you aren't authorized to be in a woman's facility."

"I apologize, my friend was throwing up, so I came in to assist her, give us a moment."

"Oh, my God! I am so fucking embarrassed right now."

"Man, fuck them people! They don't know you."

I waited until she got herself together and exited the bathroom. When we rounded the corner, people started clapping at the both of us, apparently knowing I was getting my dick sucked. I shook my head. It would've been okay if I had busted a nut. Katrina sped past me while I reached into my pocket to check who was calling me. It was a missed call and a text. The call was from a partner of mine while the text was from Keyonna. She was urging that we talk.

Keyonna:

I spoke to Ashley, and she seems concerned about the position you all are in."

I deleted the message.

"J, what up boy!" I turned to see Steve looking like he was already wasted. "Damn, bruh, you're enjoying yourself, huh?"

"Man, you already know. I'm around here chasing Kiwi ass, though."

My eyes got big at the sound of her name. She was something special in the group. Brown skinned with a body full of tattoos. She reminded me of COOKIESNTATTS except she was more intriguing, more dimensional. An ex-stripper, she was really about making moves now hosting parties and doing club promotions. My eyes scanned the place looking for her as well, because I damn sure wanted to have a conversation with her.

"She's the right one to chase, where her ass at?"

"Up in the section over there. I'm thinking about getting a room not too far at Aloft. You know we can G one or two of these hoes if you down."

"Give 'em that V.A. dick, huh, bruh?" We both laughed, giving each other dap.

"Fa sho, you already know."

"Hit my phone if you make a move before I do cause Katrina in this bitch faking. I might fuck with a snow bunny tonight, just to try some different shit."

"Man, you're lying your ass off. You ain't bout that life."

"I haven't, but I'm loving the mixture of women running around here, plus these white women got a lil ass on em."

My phone buzzed again, but this time, it said PRIVATE. I started thinking Keyonna or Ashley since I had been ignoring them both.

"Josiah, whatcha got going on? I heard you were in here being naughty?" I looked up and seen one of our members Cindy and then looked over at Steve and shook my head. "Did I not just speak that up?" She looked at the both of us waiting for an explanation. I reached out and gave her a hug.

"I'm just doing a lil meeting n' greeting, that's all."

My phone buzzed again, same thing, PRIVATE. I held up a finger indicating I'd be back, leaving Cindy and Steve to talk while I answered the call.

"HELLO!"

"It's me, Kat."

"Yo, why the hell are you calling me private?"

"I don't give this number out and my other phone is dead, but I wanted to catch you before you start trying to make moves and slide on a bitch."

"What the hell are you talking about?"

"Don't be stingy with the dick now, you got me started, and I want to finish."

I started shaking my head while looking at the ladies walk past.

"Yeah, I'm watching your ass now."

"Look, my homey might get a room that we can hit up if you tryna get down."

"Your homey?"

I could hear the sound of disappointment or disgust in her voice which didn't matter. My intentions weren't to stay in D.C. tonight anyway.

"Yeah, I wasn't planning on staying, and he got the joint in case we got too trashed to drive back."

She was quiet. It didn't matter; I was scanning the room looking for other options anyway. About an hour or so later, Steve had texted me an address informing me that the plans had changed. I stepped outside to call him because for the most part I was drinking, taking pictures and talking shit. I was ready for some different kind of entertainment.

"Bro, you are gonna want to be down for this one. And I have a surprise."

"Oh, yeah?"

I heard the voices in the background laughing.

"Say no more, I'm there."

It had only taken me about fifteen minutes to find the house. I knocked on the door and waited, then knocked again after a minute or two had passed. Beyond the door, I could hear laughter, so I called Steve again while walking towards the back of the house. The next door neighbor's security lights came on which made me pause for a second, caught off guard. Dogs began barking in the distance, and I started to think how shaky this probably looked to someone looking out of the window.

As I approached the back of the house, through one of the windows, I could hear the song, "Private Dance" along with the voice of a female talking. The nature of her conversation was hard to make out, but once I heard a male's voice I tapped on the window.

"Steve! Yo, man, unlock the door!" I yelled.

"Josiah, is that you? My bad."

I walked back to the front of the house. By the time I reached the door, Steve was standing in the doorway with a towel on and his smart phone in hand.

"It's going down bro!" he said excitedly.

We both walked down the hall to the corner room which was the bathroom, and that's when I saw both Kiwi and one of the girls from her section together in the Jacuzzi.

"Hey," they both chimed in, upon seeing me enter.

"Okay, what's happening," I replied unlacing my shoes and stripping off my clothes. I watched them as they watched me, predator versus prey. When I bent down to pull my boxer briefs to my knees and stand up so that they could fall to my ankles, Kiwi raised up out of the water.

"Come on in, Josiah."

Her nipple rings were tempting, and I knew before the night was over that I wanted to wrap my tongue around them. Hell, one of the first things I was going to do after getting in the water was to suck on them.

"Bro, you want something to drink?" Steve had asked.

"Man, I'm already feeling nice, but I'll take whatever they have."

"Kiwi, come here."

I frowned my face as I watched her get out of the water. *I know this dude isn't low key cuffin'*, I thought, especially after that Keyonna incident.

Kiwi winked, walked past and then grabbed a towel off the counter.

"Girl, bring me back a shot," the redbone in the water yelled.

I climbed in the Jacuzzi and sat behind her, "Nice spot, what's up with you?"

"It's my birthday, so it's all about me!" I didn't even know who this girl was or her name and yet the way she was looking at me said 'try me'. I reached for her to come towards me and without any further prompting she straddled me, but didn't sit down.

"This what you're looking for?" She started toying with me.

I knew she was drunk and ready to act up as I ran my hand down her stomach, looking at how hairy she was. There was hair all on her arms and her face. She had the Ashanti sideburns, thick eyebrows, and a light mustache. She was a lil sexy monster who was comfortable not shaving, not that it was out of control, it just was thicker than what I preferred. Her song played in the background as she closed her eyes and danced. I knew she saw my dick peeking out the water as I leaned my head back and reached up to touch her thighs. I wanted to fuck, get some head or something. I reached up between her legs to feel her pussy, but she grabbed my wrist stopping me before I could touch her.

"You don't get to do that. If I want to fuck then, I'll let you know. Right now I don't want your dick."

"Why is that? You into girls?"

"Cause men have too much shit with y'all, always thinking with your dicks."

"Aren't you looking to enjoy yourself one good time for your birthday, try some different shit?"

****

It was as if she had already tuned me out because she started singing that song by Dej Loaf, "You, Me & Hennessy." Kiwi was returning with the drinks when out the corner of my eye, I saw Steve grab her by the arm and pull her back to the side saying something to her. I couldn't make out what he was saying, but I did see Kiwi snatch her arm away.

"Damn bitch, you ain't showing Josiah no love!" Kiwi said sitting the drink on the floor beside the Jacuzzi.

"No love like a muthafucka." I added, my arousal already deflating. I could've gotten with Katrina.

They began talking shit to each other, whispering while Steve held his phone up.

"Bro you on Snapchat, say something."

"V-A baby, follow me at Designerswagg."

"All of us can't fit into the Jacuzzi, baby. Y'all come on into the bedroom," Kiwi suggested.

My eyes were on Kiwi just as much as hers were on me. She was wasted, but I sensed her nonverbal communication by the way our eyes lingered on one another.

As we both were about to exit the Jacuzzi, I grabbed ole girl by the waist.

"I want you to sit on this dick one good time. I'm telling you…"

"Boy, bye."

I pressed up against her, backing her against the wall doing something I didn't usually do. Having someone dismiss me as casual as she did, yet still sending me signals wasn't adding up.

"What do yo-"

"Shut the fuck up with all that damn whining," I placed my hand over her mouth. I didn't know if she was the type, but I was going to try some shit tonight. "Grab my dick, I want you to jerk that muthafucka. And you better get it hard!" I demanded.

Her eyes got as big as quarters, but she reached down and wrapped her fingers around my manhood and started caressing, pulling on me lightly. I took my hand from her mouth and leaned in beside her ear.

"Squeeze it tighter."

I started gyrating my hips getting into her rhythm. She watched me.

"Harder, jerk it!" I closed my eyes. "Shit…" When I opened them again she was biting down on her lip watching what she was doing. I reached down behind her ass and found her spot with my middle finger. She was wet and I was only massaging her lips. I could feel the difference between her being wet from the water and being wet from her arousal.

"This shit turning you on, ain't it?"

She rubbed me against her hairy pussy as I leaned down just a tad to make sure I was aligned. When I entered her, she raised up onto her tip toes.

"I haven't had a dick in almost a year," she whispered.

It felt like it because she was tight as hell. I had only pushed my way inside of her and pumped twice before I felt like I was on the verge of cumming. I tried to stop moving, but by now she was into it, so I said fuck it and kept going. After about six or seven strokes I pulled out then tried playing it off by suggesting that we hit the bedroom where it would be more comfortable. In all actuality though, my dick was shrinking, and I needed a moment to get myself back together again. Her reaction appeared to be that she was saddened by the choice, but she shrugged it off.

The bedroom was big and had a nice chocolate king size bed full of pillows. Half of them got knocked on the floor as both the birthday girl and I climbed in bed. Steve and Kiwi had stopped kissing.

"Y'all okay?" she questioned.

"Yeah, we good."

Kiwi dropped down to her knees in between Steve's and began giving him head. Reaching for the other girl, he pulled her to the edge of the bed, opened her legs wide and began eating her pussy.

Fuck! I thought. It was a moment of ultimate shock knowing I had shot a load of semen in her pussy. My eyes were big as hell, but at this point, there was nothing I could do except take it to the grave with me. Watching Kiwi give head was turning me on and getting me aroused again. I wanted to fuck her so badly, just one on one though.

"Hold on Ki, hold on," Steve called out.

"What the fuck you mean 'hold on'? You're going to stop me so that you can eat this bitch pussy."

I looked up to see Steve behind ole girl while she was on her stomach giving me head.

"What you mean? Ain't that why we here?" Steve began.

"You been in my face all night and the first chance you get to stick ya face in some pussy! It should've been mine is what the fuck I'm saying!"

"Man, you tripping right now."

"No, the fuck I'm not. I see how you've been looking at her ass when you think I am not looking."

"Kiwi, come on yo, we just having some fun." I jumped in.

"Yeah girl, it's my birthday, we've been turning up all night…"

"Nah, I'm saying if it's good for you then it should be good for me." Kiwi directed towards Steve and I knew right then what she was referring to. He pulled her out of the room to talk while the two of us lied in bed looking at each other like what the fuck just happened. The mood was dead we agreed as she got out of bed and began looking for her panties.

"See, I don't want her to think I was doing any disrespectful shit."

"They'll work that shit out," I tried redirecting her, but once she grabbed a t-shirt, she left the room.

For a moment, I lied back hearing every so often a raised voice, but I knew Kiwi was drunk and just in her feelings about something. I walked over to the corner of the room and reached into my pants pocket to grab my phone. I had several texts messages from Katrina looking for me and two missed calls, another call from PRIVATE, and a text from Keyonna. I started to go through them when Steven came around the corner, "Bruh, you ready?"

"Yeah, gimme a minute."

Kiwi came in the room, "Josiah, it's nothing against you, but ya friend is a disrespectful asshole."

I just shook my head. Everywhere I turned I was getting caught up in some drama. I was deciding in that moment to fall the hell back on a lot of shit. In the car Steve tried to make it appear that it wasn't a big deal, if we all were there to freak with each other. However, the truth I pieced together thinking back on from when I first got there was nothing but him wanting his cake and eating it too. It was cool for him to suck n' fuck, but when it came time for her wanting to kick it with me, he didn't want that.

Fifteen minutes into the trip, Steve was snoring.

I opened up my text message to a fucking sonogram picture and started shaking my head. *This girl*, I thought. After that, she sent another much lengthier text.

By the time I made it to Richmond, I was ready to go to sleep myself. I woke Steve up so he could go his way while I got myself situated, took a quick shower then climbed into bed. I welcomed the next day.

There was a loud banging on the door that woke me up. Groggily, I opened my eyes and went to open it up without checking to see who it was. On the other side, it was Keyonna forcing her way inside of my place.

"I've texted you repeatedly because I knew she would do something extreme."

"What are you talking about and how did you find out where I lived at?"

"I know people that know people."

"What's going on, what the hell you talking about?" I questioned.

"Ashley called me saying that she was coming up here, and now she isn't answering her phone."

"Y'all muthafuckas is tripping! Why is it so hard for y'all to leave me the fuck alone and go on about your business?"

"Hold the fuck up! You act like we did something to you."

"Man, just leave me the fuck alone."

Keyonna threw her hands up, shook her head and walked out.

I closed the door and went back to my bedroom. Just as I was about to lay down, I realized that I didn't park in my normal spot and fucking with these broads anything could happen.

****

"Fuck!"

I threw on some clothes and made it downstairs, but neither Keyonna nor Ashley was in sight. As I walked in the direction of where I parked my car, everything looked okay until I got closer. On the driver side was scratched "DickMan" plus there were eggs broken on top of the hood and roof. She was making sure I spent money on an entire paint job. Immediately, I went into my pocket and dialed Ashley's number. It rang three times then went to voicemail. I called again and got the same thing.

Ashley:
It doesn't feel good 2 be disregarded, huh?

Me:
Imma get some bitches from the hood to fuck U up, U done started something.

Ashley:
You wouldn't do that 2 the mother of UR child now would U?

Me:
It's fun n' games now.

Ashley:
And, I'll have the last laugh. Gotta head 2 the studio now, toodles...

It had taken a moment, but then it clicked when she said studio that she was going to my studio. I opened my Uber app and sent in my request for a car. I ran upstairs and changed my clothes, grabbed my wallet and my keys. When I got the notification that my Uber was downstairs minutes later, I headed back out. Upon my arrival at the shop everything seemed to be intact. I opened the door inside, disabled the alarm and walked around. When I saw everything was okay, I sat with my head in my hands.

How in the hell I get in this position? I thought to myself. There was knocking on the door up front, I looked and saw a man, no one I knew.

I walked to the door, but didn't open it. "What are you looking for bruh?" I asked through the glass.

"You the artist?" he questioned.

"Why, what's up?"

"You fucking with my wife!" It was as if that moment moved in slow motion, he charged forward through the glass.

I jumped, startling myself awake. I looked side to side in the dark and realized that I was in my bedroom, still lying in my bed. I sat up and shook my head. I couldn't get any peace even in my sleep. I grabbed my phone to check the time. It was after four. I opened my texts. It read: *I sent you an email.*

I took a deep breath and opened my Gmail account.

"If I'm honest with myself, I know that this baby very well is my husband's because of the math. I'm nine weeks pregnant, and I guess I just wanted the attention I thought I would get with having you back in my life all over again. Although I know we would've been great parents together, I am selfish to want you to want what I do. That being said, I'm very aware that my current situation clearly does not allow for me to even have these types of thoughts. I was vulnerable, and you came at a time when I most needed. Honestly, if things were different and I wasn't married, this would make me the happiest woman in the world because it would be an amazing symbol of our long-lasting love for each other. I don't want to bring added drama to your life, I only told Keyonna about the pregnancy because that's my girl and I no longer look at my husband as my husband. I need guidance I guess, but I'll stay in my lane."

****

Two weeks later, Steve and I were out playing basketball in

Rockwood Park when I was going down on a fast break trying to shine. Another player undercut me and caused me to come down hard on my arm. In mid-air, I knew it was going to be bad, but never did I imagine how bad when my right arm snapped like a twig. I could still hear the sound of my bones as they cracked. At first, it didn't register but the moment I looked down, I began yelling. I ended up going to the hospital which wasn't too far, where they cleaned, bandaged and set my arm in a cast. I sat numb for a while replaying what the doctor had told me behind closed doors. When I made it home, call it premonition, but as I walked inside, I was pushed from behind. Falling slightly to the ground I turned to see Keyonna holding a gun, looking as crazy as anyone I'd ever seen.

"Keyonna, what do you call yourself doing?"

"Oh, now you have conversation for me, huh?"

I tried getting up, but she raised her arm towards me.

"Go ahead, sit your ass in that chair over there, better yet, let's go to the boom-boom room where all the magic happens."

"Yo, I don't know what you want, but whatever it is, it isn't that serious."

"I've been thinking about this moment for a while now, Josiah, not knowing what I wanted to do. I've prayed about it, but I realized that I was praying for the wrong things."

I was lost. I didn't know what the hell she was talking about.

"What's the problem, Key? Because it seems as if you feel I've wronged you or some shit?"

"I've read the emails and the texts messages between you two. It's highly disrespectful for her to still have them all, but it's like she was flaunting it in my face. After all these years, she's still competing with me as if we were still in middle school."

"If you read them all, then you know how I feel."

"And, that proves what? When she plainly has said where her

heart is?"

I tried easing my hand into my pocket and making an emergency call without her noticing what I was doing. She was doing a lot of fidgeting around so I was able to get it unlock, but before I could do anything else she walked towards me.

"You think that you're the smartest cookie in the jar, huh?"

"I don't want Ashley."

"What the fuck do you mean you don't want her, when you have had her? This is what I've come up with…"

She opened the revolver and dropped all of the bullets on the floor, bent down and showed me the one that she put back. She spun the chamber and never took her eyes off of me.

"I've made peace with what I'm about to do. We are going to play a game almost like the King of the Hill. You remember that game growing up?"

"My mother was strict and didn't allow me to go outside much."

"Well, ain't that a bitch."

"I don't wanna play any games. I'm too old for 'em."

"But…you play 'em with these women! You played it with my best friend. I've watched you for the past week and a half. See no comment, huh?"

I didn't have anything to say. She wasn't going to do anything, but use it against me anyway.

"So men always get away with doing what they want when it comes to a woman's feelings. Y'all disregard us and throw us away whenever you feel like it with no repercussions. No more, not from me."

She held the gun up and spun the chamber again, pointed at me and pulled the trigger. I felt the urine run down my leg as I watched my life flash before me. She then turned the gun on herself and pulled the trigger. It just clicked. Out of nowhere she began laughing.

"Well look at that, let's try that one more time for shits and giggles."

She opened and spun the chamber just like before. This time, she came and put her face right next to my face. When she raised her arm, all I could think about was how my life was about to end this way.

"Close your eyes, Josiah."

I felt her lips touch mine and then came the gunshot.

About the Author

Meet the literary world's newest crown jewel, Justin "Q" Young, author of *Move Dat Doe* (Firstborn Publications 2014), Amazon's Best-Selling African American Erotic Short Story Series, *Dickmitized* (Firstborn Publications 2015) and *The Writer's Gift* (Firstborn Publications 2015), an anthology, *Fiyah Starter* (Kenerly Presents 2016), #BooksAreABusiness (DivaBookInc 2016), *Betrayed By Love Adored By Lies* (Firstborn Publications 2017) & The Words I Didn't Say 2 (Delphine Publications 2017) Bringing you vivid detailed imagery through his words, makes escaping into his stories effortless.

Multi-faceted in creativity, Justin "Q" Young defines the spectrum in artistic aptitude through painting, drawing and graphic design which includes, but not limited to: custom painted portraits, murals, digital book cover designs, promotional advertisements and his popular themed Paint Nights in different cities.

He is a public servant to community-based non-profit organizations, is a member of Hobson Lodge #23. He dedicates his time and resources to aid men, women and families enduring hardships with life's necessities.

To view Justin "Q" Young's work, please visit his Social Media Networks:

Facebook: Justin Q Young
2nd page: Author Q
Instagram: @firstborn_designs
Pinterest: JQYoung1976

DICKMITIZED

AccessJustinYoung@gmail.com

Artist, Author, Graphic Designer
www.firstborndesigns.com
Email: accessjustinyoung@gmail.com

Instagram: @firstborn_designs
Pinterest: JQYoung76
Facebook: JUSTIN Q YOUNG

Also check out his other titles:
MOVE DAT DOE 1.5
THE WRITER'S GIFT
QUEEN

MOVE DAT DOE

A Novel By:

Justin Q Young

JUSTIN "Q" YOUNG

Copyright 2015 by Justin Young.

This book is a work of fiction. The names, characters, places and incidents are products of the writer's imagination or have been used fictitiously and are not to be construed as real. Any resemblance to persons, living or dead, actual events, locale or organizations is entirely coincidental. All rights are reserved. No part of this book may be used or reproduced in any manner whatsoever without written permission.

ISBN (978-0-692-29065-1)

CHAPTER 1

* Quay *

I woke up this morning knowing everything had changed, and for the most part, would never be the same. Still in disbelief, trying to piece things together; I replayed last night's conversation and the series of events which unfolded.

"It was really nothing you could do…it's not your fault Q."

Sitting in my black on black S550 Mercedes, realizing I had more questions that I didn't and probably wouldn't get any answers for. Taking a deep breath, I rubbed my eyes trying to ward off an ensuing headache; wishing this situation I now found myself in could be pushed away just as easily.

The temperature display on the dash read 88 degrees, but the mid-afternoon's humidity made it feel miserably hot. Noticing the crowds of people walking pass my car, I had a thought that all good things come to an end at some point. Shuffling along in huddled groups, while a few stragglers followed from; I knew this was my cue to make my peace and say goodbye. Aaliyah's *"I Miss U"* played on repeat the entire drive. Somehow it give me the strength I needed to push forward; because emotionally I was all over the place.

I repositioned the Gucci shades resting on top head to my eyes, stepped out of my car; looking myself over for a brief moment in the reflection of the tint. My motto was always: *TO LOOK AND*

FEEL LIKE MONEY, but today I wasn't my normal cocky self; today wasn't the best of days for me. Dressed in a simple linen outfit with Gucci loafers, I knew from the outside looking in everything would appear normal; yet I was broken in a way words couldn't express.

"I can get through this," I whispered to myself walking towards the ceremony, one foot in front of the other; the sound of gravel underneath the soles of my loafers shifted and crunched. As I reached a row of fold-out chairs, I hesitated contemplating where to sit. I had no desired place, hell truth of the matter is I really didn't want to attend; but I had to be here for her. I quickly scanned the faces of those who were present, recognizing a couple of them. Those whose eyes I made contact with, I offered a polite wave. A few others who were close or had come to me, I embraced with a brief hug. I couldn't bring myself to smile, nothing about today held any resemblance of joy.

Within earshot I continuously heard "I'm sorry for your lost, or everything will get better with time." Did folks really have a clue, or were they just going through the motions of saying what's to be expected? Before I took my seat, I overheard a conversation from behind.

"Girl it's some fine brothas here, I might have to drop some tears in this muthafucka."

"I know that's right! Look over there, girl he has some shoulders I wouldn't mind leaning on."

As I turned around, the pair were giving each other a high five; snickering amongst themselves until they saw they had gotten my attention. I looked in disgust and they responded by rolling their eyes. Moving ahead two rows in an attempt to escape the ratchet girls, I couldn't help but to shake my head as I looked over the program. It was humorous in a way, I had expected some degree of phoniness; but was caught off guard by that conversation and to the degree in which some would go just to hook up.

Looking over the typed text and the design quality of the program, a habit of mine, last night's discovery replayed itself in my mind.

I had been returning some e-mails and laughing at some of my messages since changing my profile picture on Facebook. The game was on too, so my attention was split in half going from one screen to the other. Being online consumed most of my days, meeting new people, networking and trying to create new business opportunities for myself. I was finally getting a chance to really appreciate having some down time when my cell phone unexpectedly dinged on the nightstand. I picked it up without a thought, touching the face on the screen to open the text message.

~ Call me ASAP...269-6677 ~

The number didn't immediately register, but the signature that accompanied put my mind momentarily in the gutter.

TASTE MY MOCHA

Sounds of the NBA playoffs caught my attention on the 42" flat screen, which lit up my bedroom. Forgetting about the text, I damn near jumped out of bed knocking my laptop on the floor when Kyrie Irving went down clutching his leg.

"Mannnnn, hell nah this is some bullshit!"

I was instantly frustrated knowing if Kyrie went out with Kevin Love hurt as well, the chances of the Cavs getting a title this year would definitely be over. LeBron is the best player in the NBA, but he couldn't do it all by himself. I received a text from one of my best friends talking trash, he hated Lebron and his decision. I looked at the notification coming across my phone without opening the message, shaking my head at the same time.

Moving my computer from the other side of the bed, I wondered who *TASTE MY MOCHA* really was? A few possibilities came to mind, one in particular was the bartender at the night club Vanquish. What started as business venture to secure a night to put together a Denim & Diamonds party. Unexpectedly ended up with her and I flirting, coming on to each other. It had been a couple days since our last conversation, so I was excited about the opportunities that laid ahead. As I thought of who the mystery woman was, it became insignificant because whoever it was had my mind turning over some ideas; which caused me to shift the bulge in my sweatpants.

Grabbing the remote, I muted the T.V. and walked towards the living room; it held tall glass windows allowing me a panoramic view onto the streets of downtown. My phone in hand, I touched the number within the text and listening as it began ringing. I loved looking out onto the city at night, it was relaxing watching the cars and their lights; as well as the comings and goings of the many people who walked along the sidewalks to their destinations. The phone stopped ringing, I could barely hear the hello that was spoken.

"This is Q, what's up?"

A few moments passed as I sat on the edge of my sofa, I looked at the phone to make sure it hadn't lost connection. I had expected to hear a female's voice or something but found myself perplexed by the sounds of sniffling. Getting impatient and sensing a red flag, I spoke up again...

"Yo, you there?"

"I'm sorry," her voiced cracked above a whisper.

I was lost and knew without a doubt that this wasn't the shorty at the club behind the bar.

"Who is this," I questioned.

"It's Miranda Q, Nicole's friend."

"O, what's good with you?"

I sat back prepared to hear some drama, because Miranda's alternative lifestyle kept controversy.

"I don't know where to begin...so much has happened," she started.

"Take your time." I tried to reassure picking at a loose string that was on my sofa.

"Umm...Nicole OD'd Q." she spoke, barely able to finish.

"What the fuck do you mean?"

DICKMITIZED

What I was hearing didn't make sense and the look on my face couldn't register what I just heard. I began pacing back and forth in my living room, while listening to everything she was saying.

Nicole was a very close friend of mine, who'd been there for me through some of my most troubled times. We were more than friends to each other, but without the titles. She was someone who was full of life, but like everyone had her share of problems. For the most part she had done away with her demons or so I thought. Od'ing, wasn't who she was; Nicole I knew was better than this. To me, addicts were people who looked dirty, seemed to be falling apart and were unable to keep themselves together. Nicole was nothing like that; she held a respectable position with a local tax office and was doing her thing. Everyone sang her praises for the work she'd done to ensure speedy returns. Her children were her life and their happiness is what motivated her beyond measure. I began repeating those two letters over and over again in my head...O. D., unable to connect the dots. It just didn't make sense!

Miranda described how Nicole's mother found her inside of her apartment. She goes on to explain how lately things had become increasingly difficult for her. Cutting her off, I had my own questions because I didn't know the person she described.

"So look...you're tryna say Nicole took her own life, that this was something she did intentionally?"

My tone showed the frustration I felt, I didn't want to hear any speculation or hearsay; I needed facts!

"Q, I'm sorry but obviously she was overwhelmed and dealing with issues she kept from everyone."

"Man, are you serious?" I didn't want to accept what she was saying.

As Miranda and I continued to talk, she revealed to me what only a couple people knew what Nicole had been dealing with in regards to her health. As depressing as it was, I found myself unable to finish watching the game, or doing anything else for that matter. I don't know exactly when I hung up the phone, time seemed to move faster than usual and I lost track of time staring off into the night.

Sitting a couple feet from her casket, I thought about all the questions I wouldn't get answers to. The preacher began to speak on faith and adversity.

"Psalm 30:5 says, "weeping may endure for a night, but joy comes in the morning. This too shall pass where we will move from our sadness and move towards all of the memories that brought us joy, amen."

Everyone agreed in unison with amen, or nodding their heads. He pointed to Nicole's portrait and at that moment it became so surreal for me. Nicole, 34 years old, the mother of three beautiful daughters; who was loving, unselfish and worthy of so much more was indeed gone. The preacher continued to offer words of comfort, sobs filled the air and loved ones embraced each other. A voice from behind me began singing without any prompt, "His eyes are on the sparrow;" I continued to look at the smile in the portrait.

Her smile took me back, I couldn't help but to reminisce on what once was. Nicole and I hit it off from the moment we'd met. It was like we had known each other for years.

The fact that she killed herself started to bother me again, I watched people slowly begin paying their last respects; leaving flowers on her casket and whispering their last heart felt words. I knew her daughters would take this the hardest, I looked over and watched them as they were being rocked by their grandmother. A few of Nicole's friends said their tearful goodbyes, all of them seemed deeply pained by her death. I wondered if they knew she contracted H.I.V., would that change their disposition of her, who would help and who would abandon her. Did she think that I would, why didn't she at least give me a chance to be there for her?

Nicole's brother held the hands of her two youngest daughters and encouraged them to say "bye-bye to mommy." Already distraught, he was taking this tragedy harder than the children. I moved closer, to my surprise Nicole's brother pushed the picture and the flowers off the top of the casket; trying to open it. His behavior shocked everyone and made me wonder what in the world had gotten into him?

I found myself standing up, stuck as a few bystanders attempted to calm Nicole's brother; who was refusing to allow anyone to get close to him. The preacher even backed away, sensing how out of control things had become.

"Who plans to stop me from telling my sister goodbye," he shouted through clinched teeth. The darkness of his facial expressions showed that he had lost it.

I understood goodbyes, I knew everyone handled grief differently; maybe this was his way of coming to terms with her death and gaining closure. I even wished I could see Nicole one last time or been able to give her the comfort she so desperately needed.

Her daughters and others cried, holding their heads down as Nicole laid in the casket exposed. Seeing her that way made me look away, not because I was weak or couldn't take it; but because I didn't want that to be the lasting image on my mind of her. I moved a couple of chairs to the side reaching Nicole's brother, who was now on his knees. I touched his shoulder to get his attention, not trying to stop him from making his peace; but hoping that I could get him to see that there was a better way.

"We all love her man, but look..." I turned to show him the mess he caused emotionally and physically.

"She doesn't deserve to be remembered like this."

On his knees looking up at me with tears flowing from his eyes and his body shaking with emotions, he apologized.

"I'm so sorry baby girl, I'm so sorry."

I reached over and closed the top of the casket, pausing for a second to say my goodbye.

"Nic, this wasn't supposed to happen like this, we were

supposed to grow old together. I feel this is partly my fault because of how busy I've been. I was so caught up in my own world that I didn't see that you needed me; I am sorry for that. You meant more to me than I showed at times, and I guess I took you for granted; thinking we'd always have time to get to us."

I wanted to continue but with the lump that was starting to swell up in my throat, the words were starting to become harder and harder to speak. I touched my lips, then her casket; said my final goodbye and made my exit. Before leaving, I turned to face her daughters who I hugged and kissed. Her mother held me tight and repeated in my ear, "There's no more we can do for her. She's with God now."

I couldn't speak so I just shook my head in agreement, I put my shades on to hide the ensuing tears and headed towards my car. I got in my car and closed the door, I could no longer hold back my tears and for the first time, I cried.

CHAPTER 2

* Phil / Six*

The moment I saw the blue sign on the side of the highway that read "Welcome to Virginia", I felt relieved that I'd finally made it. The past couple of hours had me questioning this whole trip, I was sick of being cooped up inside this car, sick of being on the road surrounded by all of this unfamiliarity and sick of hearing the annoying voice coming from the GPS.

Watching the speedometer, I couldn't help but to be cautious and on the lookout for state troopers. Having out of state license plates, made me feel like a flashing neon sign down the highway; as police oftentimes use that as an excuse to pull drivers over. Lately the attitude of law enforcement concerning black men hasn't been the best. I wanted to avoid any confrontation at all costs.

Colorado was now thousands of miles in my rear view and I intended to do everything to keep it that way. Even though I was agitated with being in the car, it was far better than being locked up in a small ass jail cell. In my head all I kept thinking was, "just a little bit longer and I'll be in the arms of my girls," referring to my daughter and her mother Dawn.

For a while she'd been making her plea for us to, "live as a family and for me to choose a better lifestyle." I wasn't against slowing down and doing the family thing. I just had to put it in a timetable that was manageable for what I had going on. When I arrived today I suspected that she would be pleasantly surprised; seeing this as a move in the right direction. Though it would be nice if it was only that, but I had ulterior motives I wasn't proud of. However, this was the dilemma I was in.

Due to my impulsiveness, my rep in the streets had my name buzzing. I had to lay low for a while, somewhere far and it only made sense for it to be close to my daughter in the event that something happened. Hard as it was for me to admit, I realized that my attitude and ego needed correcting.

In my passenger seat were a variety of miscellaneous junk food wrappers and containers, an unusual sight but these were unusual circumstances. Pushing everything on the floor to retrieve my cell phone, I held it above the steering wheel so that I could pick through the menu options and drive at the same time.

~ I gotta surprise 4 u ~

Sending Dawn a text would be far easier than calling; because knowing her, she would have a million and one questions. Our relationship over the years had its ups and downs, but even with me running the streets or dealing with other chicks, she endured and remained by my side.

From the time we met she carried herself differently than most, almost with a degree of naivety. I introduced myself as "Six", a nickname I was known for in the streets. I remembered her looking at me sideways cutting her eyes at me and responding with:

"What's the name your mother gave you?"

"Damn, you want a niguhs government," I said laughing.

"I'm not the police, nor do I work for social services; so what's the problem?" She questioned with a straight face with hands on her hips in a matter of fact manner.

For a moment I paused, taking in not just what she'd come back at me with, but the manner in which she had done so. With a smile I responded,

"Phil, my mother named me Phil."

Traffic slowed down drastically, as I passed construction workers in bright orange vests. I began to see signs that were posted informing drivers to merge lanes. I had gone from doing 85 mph on highway 85, to now moving 5 mph; I was beginning to get impatient. Allowing the car beside me to squeeze in front, the driver gave me thumbs up out of his window. Noticing the bullet holes in my dash, I was reminded how they got there and what triggered the events that happened soon thereafter as I slowly inched forward passing the highway workers repaving the road.

A couple of Dawn's girlfriends had thrown together a celebration party to congratulate her on her new job. Leaving to go to Virginia and not knowing when exactly she would make it back because of her schedule; they all set out to have a girl's night out. I won't trip about the partying, although I still hadn't gotten over how she sprung on me that this job would be taking her and my daughter to the east coast. Knowing that this move would put a strain on the relationship between my daughter and I made me more than salty. Considering doing my own thing, I decided to invite a couple of my boys for drinks.

Throwing on a throwback Tampa Bay Bucs snapback along with a white T-shirt and some Levi's- I kept it simple. My jewelry game was crazy so there wasn't a need to be too over the top when I was on chill mode.

As I made my way to the lounge, I hadn't even parked yet before noticing how long the line was. The guys on one side, the ladies on the other, I just knew with this amount of people some drama would pop off; especially with how slow the line was moving.

"What the fuck!!!" "Who is he?" "That's that bullshit right there!" I heard from behind as I approached my homeboy who worked the door as security.

"What's good bruh?"

"Man, I can't call it. You know you're good though." He said motioning me inside.

Once in, I still had to pass another set of doors before entering the main floor area. Taking that time to text my boys that I had made it, I wasted no time entering and seeing how jammed packed the place really was. Bodies were wall to wall, pressed against each other from the dance floor to the bar. Rick Ross and Wale's song had everybody feeling it, "my bitch bad looking like a bag of money."

As I snaked my way to get some drinks, I could smell the aroma of each female I passed as different ones reached out trying to get my attention. Being in the club 5 minutes and not yet knowing where Dawn and her peoples were at; I didn't want to entertain anything without first playing it safe. So I nodded my head or motioned that I'd be back to the women I met in passing.

Not until I reached the bar did I notice in the V.I.P. section above Dawn and her group dancing; and carrying on amongst themselves. I saw Dawn before she left my place, so the dress she wore was no surprise; however, the way she was moving in it, swaying to the beat of the music had me ready to end the night early. 'I definitely was going to enjoy getting her out of those clothes,' I thought to myself.

Seeing the lustful faces of the dudes in here were kind of humorous, you could tell who were plotting to holla at a woman with intent to take them home. I noticed some individuals checking out either Dawn or somebody in her group. It wasn't long before one got up enough courage to approach, bypassing the girls closest to him and stopping at Dawn putting his hand on her lower back. I saw him whispering something in her ear, she shook her head in a 'no' response and he walked away rejected; but not before trying to do the same with someone else in the group. 'Niguhs these days be thirsty as hell,' I thought. 'He wasn't even wrong for attempting, I'll give him that.' I turned to the bartender and placed my order. "Yo let me get 2 shots of Patron, a Red bull and Vodka;" this was my usual.

My phone vibrated in my pocket, I was hoping it was Kareem and them saying they were here. I read the text then looked up at Dawn's area. She sent the message and I wondered if she'd seen me.

~ I wanna be bad w/ u 2nite ~

~ U must've been reading my mind! ~ I responded back quickly.

"Excuse me boo," a female voice said as I turned to look at who had just *bumped up against me.*

"It's cool," I responded putting my phone back into my pocket and checking her out. She went back to dancing winding her body to the rhythm of the dancehall music that was playing. I sipped on my drink and watched how the pants she wore hugged her every curve. Our eyes met more than once and I made sure she knew she had my attention. Backing up against me she rocked, dipped and threw her hair from one side to the other. I don't know if it was the drinks that were starting to take effect, the blunt I had blew earlier, the music or this woman; but I was feeling it as I pulled my hat further down on my face. I placed my hand across her stomach, pulling her closer to me and began dancing right along with her.

She was soft, gorgeous and sweat smelling. The way she leaned in inches from my face I not only smelled her perfume but could feel her breathing against my skin. The combination of the two excited me and momentarily I forgot where I was.

"You aight," she questioned backing up a little with her eyebrow half raised. It was apparent she had felt the beginnings of my arousal.

"Damn you had me lost in a moment," I confessed.

"I'll let you get yourself together then," she said almost turning to leave.

Reaching out I grabbing her wrist, I had to stop her and offer her a drink. She came closely and spoke,

"I just want to dance boo, that's all I'm here for."

As the D.J. began mixing a series of songs, I pulled her to the side of the bar where the lighting was dimmer and I could feel a bit more comfortable. Dawn was bourgeois, with a little bit of hood and plenty of Jesus. I definitely didn't want to throw it in her face what I was thinking of doing with and to this young lady.

Her features hinted that she was mixed with multiple ethnicities, slanted eyes, thick lips, dark skinned and had an accent. I wanted to ask her about herself; but didn't want to run her off. Instead I just pulled her close and we danced for a moment looking at each other, smiling periodically. Some things can be exchanged between two people without saying a word and our chemistry at that moment was captivating as I started doing my lil two step. She shook her head smiling, one thing was for certain, and she didn't leave though.

My phone caught us both off guard, as the vibration in my pocket made her jump back.

~Where u @ ~ the text message read.

~N back by the bar ~ I typed back and then leaned close to her ear.

"I'm waiting on my boys to meet me up here," I spoke while rubbing the side of her thighs. Out of nowhere an Asian female approached and quickly grabbed her by the arm. I grabbed the other out of reflex wanting to know what was going on and if she was cool. Turning her head to me she lightly pulled away,

"That's my girl," she said.

They began talking amongst each other while her Asian friend looked me over suspiciously. I just smirked at her, thinking this lil gay girl really wanted a problem? Handing over her clutch purse they both turned to leave.

"Give me your info so we can link up later." I said not wanting her to get too far.

"I didn't come here to hook up baby, sorry." She answered pouting her lips.

"Yo you just was grinding da fuck outta me . . . that's crazy!" I replied with a little smile on my face shaking my head from side to side.

Her Asian friend gave me plenty of shade by the looked at me. I thought for a moment that this might be her girlfriend I was hitting on; but then I dismissed it because she would've said something I figured. Giving in she grabbed my phone that I held out to her and began typing.

"Carress?" I said reading the name when she handed me back my iPhone.

"Yeah hit me up tomorrow, we have to get back on base."

"Oh, aight. I got you." Realizing what the rush was about.

"Be safe." she said before she turned to leave.

As I walked back toward the bar I took a quick glance up in the V.I.P. section. One of Dawn's friends looked to have been arguing with someone as another female stood in front of her to hold her back. I couldn't see what was going on, due to being one level below and poor lighting; but I've been in the streets long enough to be able to read body language.

Pushing my way towards the steps, my boys ran into me.

"What's poppin?" Kareem said all hype; yet, sensing the expression I wore on my face.

"Yo, yo, man its crazy in here tonight. Let me go check this shit out up here to make sure Dawn is straight," I said to the group.

Right behind me, they followed as I zig-zagged up the steps. Coming down, a couple dudes were laughing, "Fuck them wack ass hoes;" I overheard one of them say. In the distance I saw one of the females wiping herself off. It looked like, but I wasn't for certain, that something was thrown on her. Dawn clearly was upset trying to assist her friend so without thinking, I turned around to catch up with whom I suspected of causing the trouble.

The lights in the club pulsated making everything appear to move in slow motion. I tucked my chains within my shirt, adrenaline already pumping as I caught up with the group. I took aim for the one who I heard make the comments. I punched him dead in his shit, the others attempted to stop me but got thrown to the side; I was swinging like vintage Ali.

"Yooo!!!" voices yelled. Arms went up defensively trying to stop the punches while grabbing me. Kareem and his boys followed through I noticed out of the corner of my eye. The flickering lights within the club made it hard to see who was who but once the fight broke out everyone close by got out of the way and had their cellphones out. As I tussled with the one guy getting the best of him, outta nowhere I fell to the ground. Someone had hit me with what felt like a bottle. I tried to gather myself, get my bearings when an arm went around my neck and I was pulled to my feet. Trying to maneuver my body out of the strangle-hold, I saw the area full of black shirts that bore SECURITY in bold white lettering.

"Get the fuck off me!"

I was yelling, unable to walk on my own. I was being manhandled as if I were a small child, being taken out of the club. Pushing the door open, he released me saying,

"Don't bring that shit back up in here!"

I turned to face him, heated that my shirt was stained and disheveled. One of my chains felt like it might have been broken.

"That big shit don't mean nothing to me," I said with malicious intent, knowing it only took a little over 6 lbs. of pressure to knock a muthafuckas dick in the dirt, muscles and all. My trigger finger was all the muscles I needed.

He only grunted, turning to close the door, Dawn and her girl stepped from behind him screaming in my direction.

"What the fuck is wrong with you?"

"What!" Confused and dumbfounded, I checked my pockets for my phone. My chain had been broken, but luckily it had gotten caught within my shirt.

"I came to help y'all out, because it seemed like dude had been fucking with you n ya girls!"

"He was showing off and beefin with the girls at the table across from us Phil..." she began "... I was trippin because once he started getting out of control I didn't want him to get anyone in my party wet, but he ended up getting some shit on Precious."

In disbelief I stared at her angrily for putting myself out there for nothing.

"Are you serious?"

"It didn't have to escalate to this is all I'm saying," she went on.

Walking to the parking deck, my thoughts were on getting to my car. A situation like this was certain to have some gunplay involved, knowing how dudes be quick to get in their feelings; I didn't want to get caught out there without being strapped. Stomping behind me still complaining about her night being messed up, her friend on the cell phone giving whoever the person is a play by play detailed account of what happened. I stopped and turned around facing them both.

"Look, just go home then if you feel like that."

"No, I am not!"

"Whatchu gonna do then," I questioned.

"I'm coming with you."

"Nah, that's not gonna happen. I don't want you to get caught up if some shit pop off."

"We both can go home then," she replied.

DICKMITIZED

"Not right now, Kareem and em' are out here somewhere and I gotta make sure they're straight since I got them involved in this bullshit tonight."

"You can call him, what's wrong with your phone?"

Her girl stood there now off her phone, but with her arms crossed looking pissed. If looks could kill I probably would've been scared, but instead I just smirked. The ambiance outside wasn't any different from when I first came, but I still was on high alert. Some people walked passed us, as cars blew their horns driving by with the music blaring. My intentions still were to get to the parking deck where my car was parked. We stood damn near in the middle of the street in somewhat of a stalemate. She wasn't coming with me, I was certain of that.

"Look just get her to take you home aight." Digging in my pockets for some money to compensate her friend, she snatched the money away and began to say something; but I turned and crossed the street not giving her a chance.

Inside the parking deck I went into the stairwell, taking the steps two at a time until I got to the 3rd level. The night was quiet, but I still kept an eye out on my surroundings. By the time I reached my old skool 69" Buick Skylark, I felt a little more comfortable because I always kept my .40 caliber on the top of the front tire out of sight. No one would ever expect to look for a gun there; plus you never knew what situation would present itself so I always stay strapped.

Opening the car door, I climbed in and turned the ignition while my phone continued vibrating. On the screen Dawn's face appeared, I pushed ignore and scrolled to Kareem's number. Ringing once then going to voicemail, I slowly drove towards the lower level. The constant buzzing of my phone was becoming aggravating, as each time I looked I saw Dawn's face being the only one calling. Already registering 6 missed calls, I was prepared to tell her to calm down, but my concern was for my homeboy's welfare, making sure everybody was okay.

At the exit, I gave the attendant my stub, as I paid the fees she did a double take looking at me crazily. I thought for a second she was bugging out because the blood she was seeing on my shirt, but as I pulled away I realized the .40 caliber was sitting on my lap in plain view.

Trying Kareem's number again, this time he answered.

"What's up homey you good," he questioned.

"Man, are y'all good that's the question?"

"No doubt. You said we was gonna have some drinks not tear these muthafuckas club up.," he responded laughing.

"Man that shit is my fault, I thought niguhs was messing with my peoples and you know how I get bout her. Fuck that!"

"True. So what you bout to get into then cause the night is still early," he asked.

"The way Dawn is blowing my phone up, my night is over."

"Yeah fa sho. Hit me up then."

"Aight. Be safe."

As I sat waiting for the red light to change, out of the corner of my eye I saw an image running up to my car and fast. As I made out what he had on and holding, glass shattered everywhere. Out of instinct I threw my arm up over my face and tried ducking as best as I could while stepping on the gas pedal.

My car flew through the intersection as cars blew their horns upset, but unknowingly aware of what was occurring. Shaking the glass fragments off of my clothing, I reached for my gun that had fallen to my feet. In the rearview I saw the figure run towards an awaiting car and jumped in going in the opposite direction. That was no doubt one of the dudes from the club. Without hesitating, I bust a U-turn in the middle of the street not caring who was around and did my best to catch up with the coupe.

With one hand gripping the steering wheel, my other hand on the gun, and my foot pressed heavily on the gas; my focus was the brake lights of the cars ahead as I weaved in and around cars trying to make up ground and get closer.

Up ahead the cars looked the same but there was one whose movements mirrored mine, so I knew that was the vehicle to follow. I did my best to drive through the intersection without causing injury. A few light changes almost stopped me, but I was determined to blow pass them anyway. Catching up on a street I held the gun out of the window and just started firing.

Baca! Baca! Baca!

The coupe's back window shattered just as the driver turned a corner sharply. When I tried to make the same turn I had to slow down because of an *oncoming vehicle approaching. People began to run and duck as I continued let 3 more shots rang out. In the distance I could hear sirens, whether they were for me or not I didn't know, but I didn't want to find out neither. Reluctantly I gave up chase knowing that by now I could never catch up with the car I was chasing.*

"Damn them niguhs put holes in you baby," I said to my car rubbing the dash.

Now in Virginia, I checked my watch, only another hour and a half to go before I would reach my destination. I didn't know exactly where I was, looking out of my window only to seeing farm land as far as the eye could see. No malls or stores I was used to, just grocery stores here and there and a few Dollar Generals.

Up ahead there was a McDonalds and I wasted no time turning on my blinker so that I could make a quick pit stop. The bathroom was calling for me to blow it up. As I turned in my phone began ringing. In one fluid motion I answered while backing up to park.

"Hey ma, how are you?"

"Just checking in with you to see how you are coming along. I had another visit earlier today," she said

"O yeah, anybody I know?"

"Just the same people who always come around asking a million questions."

Inadvertently my paced slowed down to McDonalds as if I was walking towards my mother's house seeing who she was referring to.

They said that they "only wanted to ask me a few questions," but I saw too many episodes of 'The First 48' to not know better, she commented.

"I don't know what to tell you ma." Detectives I knew could be a nuisance.

"Baby I understand you're out there doing what you feel you gotta do. All I suggest that you do is keep my grandbaby in mind."

"Come on ma..." I began, but was cut off.

"You have a beautiful child Phil and a woman who has stayed by you through a lot of your foolishness..."

"Ma...!"

I knew she meant well, but was for certain the detectives had used a scare tactic making things appear worse than what they were.

"Everything is gonna work itself out," I assured her.

My mother was once in the streets so she was no stranger to the politics of them, but once she became saved, she dedicated her life to the church full time separating herself from the life she once led and the people she affiliated with.

By the time I finished using the bathroom, washed my hands and headed for the counter; I seen a couple people standing by my car as well as a police cruiser parked right beside it.

"Just my muthafuckin luck!" I mumbled watching from the window. As hungry as I was, if anything was gonna go down it was gonna go with me having a full stomach.

"Yes can I get a large Big Mac meal for here please?"

CHAPTER 3

* Dawn*

"I don't think he has any clue on what's going on in this relationship, one minute he's in tune, the next, girl, I don't know."

"Been there done that and I'm just as tired as you are." Lynn responded back.

"These brothers need to get their shit together..." I hadn't finished typing my message to her before another came in interrupting what I was in the process of saying.

"Ya man, my man and half these young dudes out here... all they want to do is sit in front of that damn playstation, run the streets, smoke and beg a bitch for some pussy."

As frustrating as it was, I had to shake my head at my girl for what she had just typed on instant message because without her really knowing the dynamics of my relationship she was describing it to a T.

I sat and staring at the computer screen looking over our conversation for the past half hour, knowing I needed to get my paperwork together for my up-coming appointment. With as much time I've invested in this account I needed to bring this one in particular to a close, because of the mixed emotions I was to feeling. As I pulled up the file and printed off the final edit, I glanced at my watch to keep track of the time not wanting to rush. With most of the account executives still at lunch, the office was very much deserted. I took opportunities like this to catch up with my girl back home, staying connected with what was happening in her world and get all the gossip she was certainly willing to share.

My circle of friends had been the same since high school, with all of us keeping in touch via phone call or email. By some of us taking careers in other states, it was kinda difficult to hang out like we use to so this was our way of making up. After throwing the files in my briefcase, I scooted back to my desk and began typing.

"So when do you admit to yourself that what you want isn't happening?"

I stared at the question a moment before hitting enter. I realized my situation was nothing short of a roller coaster ride. If it wasn't for my daughter and what I wanted her to have, my ass would've been in the wind. Here I was 31 years old dealing with a 26 old man who wasn't mature enough to see that I was everything he needed. He tried at times, we both did but for him the streets were more important and his name in them. The security he provided was comforting and I had become accustomed to the lavish lifestyle but it came with a lot of sleepless nights and constant drama. I paid the price time after time playing the role of his fool.

The computer chimed alerting a new message.

"Dawn, you my girl and fo'real at this point in your life you need to be putting your needs first."

[New message] "I'm so on the fence right now that the next thing that smells like some bullshit might just send me to someone else's yard...lol"

"YOU A MESS!" I typed.

[New message] "Girl, why Mark had pictures of some skinny ass bitch in his phone?"

I had to reread the I.M. twice because I couldn't believe the perfect couple was having problems. Having been married a couple years, their relationship was the envy of all of us just by the way they appeared to get along. Now intrigued I had to find out what was going on.

"Who? And how did you find them," I typed.

[New message] "His ex, out of curiosity I went through his phone when he came home the other night."

Shaking my head I typed, "You know what happens when you go looking for shit...you end up finding it.

[New message] "Girl please, I'ma check his phone and if he starts to really act shaky, I'ma check and smell them underwear."

[New message] "I just thought it was strange that his call log was empty know what I'm saying."

"Okay so..."

[New message] "Empty like he hadn't been on the phone all day and the way his ass talk, girl the devil is a liar!"

[New message] "Empty like he purposely deleted it because he had something to hide."

[New message] "Empty like his brain if he thinks I'ma fool and was just gonna stand by and let that go down."

"What did you do?" I typed.

[New message] "He talking about she just sent it to him out the blue. Bitches out here are thirsty and disrespectful I know, but I am not a damn fool. Boy bye!"

"I'm sure you're upset but Mark loves and adores you. You know how men can be, you said it yourself."

I was trying to get her to see things differently because men and porn kinda went hand in hand in some respect, but at least she was in a committed relationship. I wanted to be in her position, having a ring at least. I didn't want to tell her I had been down that road with the pictures. Hell, I had even had a girl pull up on me saying she was pregnant by my man and I still stayed by him. Like her though, I had no strength to fight, play games or play detective. I took this job offer with the thought in mind that some distance would be best, stepping out and away from a situation with the hopes that I would receive better clarity.

Time was getting away from me as I thought about my appointment and as the office began filling back up. Bringing our conversation to a close, I told Lynn I would get back with her, but to stay encouraged. Shutting the computer down, I grabbed my Michael Kors bag, applied a fresh coat of Mac lipstick, sprayed on some J'adore, double checked everything and headed to the elevator with attaché case in hand.

Being in Virginia, away from all of the constant reminders of Phil's infidelities was refreshing. This was the start that I needed to mentally and emotionally to put my head in its proper space. I spent some quality time decorating my townhouse, developed some new routines, formed some close associations and invested in my daughter's stability just as well. Though Phil and I talked or texted each other pretty frequently, I felt more than anything this time a part would give us the clarity we needed to shift some things in our relationship.

As I drove down the highway, I couldn't help but to remember what happened 3 years ago when we hit a crossroad in this relationship. *Unexpectedly, I became pregnant and everyone was in my ear trying to tell me then that I should know better and how I shouldn't expect this baby to change Phil's personality. "Move on with someone you can build a life with," they said.*

As emotional as the situation was already I was torn on what to do. I drove to Phil's apartment at the time prepared to make a decision based on his reaction. His response was nothing I had expected as he cried tears of joy, holding on to me repeatedly saying how much he loved me and vowed to do better in regards to us. As we made love that night, there was no way I could imagine turning my back on the possibilities our future held. I committed myself to our relationship and disregarded the whisperings around the salon and the streets that claimed Phil was laying up with this or that woman.

DICKMITIZED

Haters is what they were and stealing my joy was something I wasn't going to allow. The pregnancy had been wonderful with Phil attending every appointment and being as attentive as he was. However there was a change in him once our daughter Anya came into the world. Old habits resurfaced and his behavior became more stand-offish. I couldn't understand it nor would he explain to me if I was doing anything wrong. I became so self-conscious and weak from the rejection. Since Anya's birth we have been on again off again, so much that I felt that if he was serious about us being a family he would make the decision. Right now though, I was all for doing me because he was surely doing him.

Grabbing my Galaxy off of the seat, I sent my client Peter a text message informing him that I was nearby. Searching for decent parking would be the next obstacle as I circled the lot looking for adequate spacing. It was still lunch time for some obviously, due to the lack of spaces available. I tried not to become irritated keeping this thought in mind.

Shortly thereafter I walked into the lobby of the Hilton Garden Inn. Taking my designer shades off, I looked to see at what direction the bar was, thinking Peter surely would be waiting there. When I heard his distinguished laugh coming from the opposite direction, I turned finding him in the midst of a couple of other gentlemen in business attire further in the vestibule looking over some paperwork. Wrapping up his conversation, he pulled from his suit a couple of business cards and handed them to each person seated. When our eyes met, he smiled and began walking towards me.

When he got within arm's reach, he extended himself and we briefly hugged.

"Don't ever underestimate the power of networking or the ability to be of service to someone," he said as we separated. His cologne was intoxicating and for a moment I felt a sense of weakness, as I opened my eyes shaking my head in agreement.

"I'll keep that in mind," I responded.

A commonplace for representatives to conduct business, host various work events and networking gatherings, we both found seating nearby as others milled around.

"I brought over the contracts for you to sign off on, I also made the modifications you were concerned about."

"You didn't have to go through the trouble of bringing them, you could've sent them by courier," he said.

Taking a deep breath, I looked back at the paperwork then up at him.

"I know, but I think we should bring what we've been doing to a close and move on."

Our meetings had become something that I had looked forward to, a much needed distraction in the wake of my on again off again relationship. Our conversations were interesting and entertaining, in him I'd seen qualities I wanted all the time. He wasn't pushy or appearing to have any ulterior motives so it was easy and comfortable having my guard down.

"I have an idea if you will trust me enough to follow me."

I looked into his light colored eyes and without second guessing, shook my head in agreement. We walked in silence down the hall and into the elevator. My heart began racing as all kinds of thoughts ran through my mind about this man. He stood in front of me with such broad shoulders. I had a moment of weakness envisioning walking up behind him, wrapping my arms around his waist and just resting my head on his back.

Peter turned giving me a quick smile before the elevator door pinged and opened. I could've gotten his signature and been done, could've turned my back; but part of me wanted to be taken away by the fantasy that this was real and that he belonged to me. The past couple of days we had been talking on the phone about what we wanted in our lives. Working on a few ad campaigns had allowed me to see into his business and into his business mind; it gave me the opportunity to listen to what he was passionate about and it made me open up as well about myself. I missed feeling like an intelligent woman and longed to be held and treated as such.

Now I was here, we approached the door to the suite and we both paused for a moment before he slid the key card down the slot. I walked in knowing full well what was about to happen but before the door could close completely, Peter grabbed my wrist pulling me to him. He pressed his lips against mines, held my body close to his and as hard as my heart was beating, I melted. 'What was I doing,' I began thinking about to pull away, but my body and mind weren't in sync.

"It's okay," he whispered in my ear attempting to settle me down.

I closed my eyes and went with it. Wherever this moment was going to lead, I was willing to go. His tongue in my mouth tasted like peppermints as we kissed and fondled each other like two possessed teenagers discovering each other for the first time. My breasts were screaming to be touched and played with by hands other than my own. Before I could fully un-button my blouse, he had lifted me against the wall. I felt how hard he was against my leg as he pressed his self against me teasing and whispering in my ear how he 'wanted my pussy.' Pulling my top off, my breast sat exposed. I was only a small B cup in size but the way he cupped them both in his hands and put them in his mouth, I could see size didn't matter. My excitement only increased as he turned me on more and more watching him suck and lick on each of my nipples.

"Mmmmm," I couldn't help but to moan and hold onto the back of his head. My pussy throbbed as he slipped his hand underneath my skirt pulling to the side of my Victoria Secret panties.

'Yesssss,' I was thinking, pulling the bottom of my skirt up higher so he could get to where I needed him to be with no interference. The moment I felt his finger inside of me, I couldn't help but to wrap my arms around him tighter, as I felt on the verge of climaxing.

Biting down on my lip, I grinded against his finger as the pressure mounted. He was saying something but I was lost in my own world. My eyes were closed and though I was here with him, my thoughts were somewhere else, with someone else. That lasted only momentarily though before I completely shut that out as well.

We moved to the bed stopping briefly only to get free from our clothing. As I lay back exposing my freshly trimmed pussy waiting for him, I ran my fingers over my lips exposing how wet I was. I was so aroused, I had surprised myself by how my fingers glistened with my juices. Half expecting him to be ready with a condom in hand, he stood at the edge of the bed watching me and beating his what appeared to be limp dick apologizing.

"I'm sorry baby; I was so excited I came."

"What?" Frowning my face not believing what I had just heard. He hadn't even put it inside of me; you have got to be kidding me right now I was thinking.

"Why don't you come over here and help me Dawn," he tried to encourage.

"If your hand can't do it, I doubt mines can." I responded sarcastically.

"Maybe if you kiss on it or something you know…" he pleaded standing at the foot of the bed still stroking himself.

I know he wasn't seriously asking me to suck his dick on the low. I was feeling some type of way, looking at how limp his pink flesh laid and how crazy it was for me after all these years of being with black men, to want to try something different. The moment was definitely gone for me. I was always told that I did a poor job at concealing how I felt because my facial expressions gave me away.

Instead of looking at him in disgust right at that moment, I reached for my belongings.

"I'm sorry." I responded.

I picked up my things and headed towards the bathroom to clean myself up. This was unbelievable and for a few moments I sat on the edge of the bath-tub with my head in my lap.

"Are you okay," he asked through the door.

"Yes, I'm fine." He began to try explaining his self, but I rose up and cut the faucet on in an attempt to drown out his noise and hoping that he would get the message how disappointed I was about this whole thing. I looked into the mirror, I could only shake my head about the position I'd just put myself in. I should've known this would've been too good to be true.

By the time I exited the bathroom, he was gone and the contracts sat signed on the bed along with a short note.

'I can make up for this if you allow me...' it started, but without finishing it I balled the paper up and threw it in the waste basket.

I walked out of the suite looking at my watch and straightening my clothes; waiting on the elevator doors to open. Thinking now I could go pick my daughter from daycare, I pulled my phone from my purse and saw I had a message.

~ *I gotta surprise 4 u* ~

Phil had texted over an hour ago. I felt a tinge of guilt knowing what just occurred, but responded with a few question marks instead.

Once I made it to the daycare my head was clear, putting the last 45 minutes behind me. Walking up to the entrance, I did the usual, punched the access code into the keypad, signed Anya out then walked to her classroom. She and a few other children sat in groups eating cookies and popcorn while telling each other stories. The laughter of children instantly made me smile.

"Hey Chico." I called out, a nick-name I had given her

because of how skinny, but adorable she was.

"Mommy," she sung out and ran to my open arms giving me kisses and hugs.

"Get your things so we can go, hey you guys." I waved at the other kids who were around Anya.

"They gotta sit over there by themselves because they are messy and spill things." One child tapped me on my leg to say, he was pointing at 3 boys who look like Kool- Aid was everywhere, but there cups.

"Awwww look at them," I commented to the teacher.

"Girl, those three are a t-r-i-p," she spelled out shaking her head and rolling her eyes.

"I can imagine."

Minutes later we were back in the car and on our way home finally. This had been a long day, I just wanted to relax, drink me some wine and catch the new episode of POWER that was On-Demand.

"Mommy I want something to eat!" Anya demanded from the back when she saw the golden arches of McDonalds.

"We're almost home now don't you want to wait," I tried negotiating. I was hungry myself and not really feeling up to cooking.

"Please mommy," she whined.

I looked back at Anya before turning into the drive thru. McDonalds did sound good right about now. I ordered 2 chicken nugget happy meals digging in after paying and pulling off from the window. Watching In the rearview as Anya bopped her head to the music while holding a nugget in one hand and fries in another; singing Silento's chorus that was playing on the radio.

"Watch me whip, whip, watch me Nae Nae."

She could be so grown at times. At the light I checked my cell phone to see if Phil had sent me any new messages.

~ You'll see ~

I pulled into the parking lot of my townhouse, immediately I started smiling because there he was old skool and all in front of my house.

"Anya your daddy is here!" I said in disbelief.

"My daddy?" She said just as surprised as I was.

Excited, I felt butterflies in my stomach. It had been more than a couple of months since we'd seen each other; how ironic that today of all days he decides to pop up I thought. As I parked, Phil got outta his car smiling.

"Surprise, hey baby," he kissed me and turned to get Anya outta the back seat.

"What, that's all I get after all this time? Negro you better get over here and hug me like you miss me."

Bear hugging me and swinging me around, my happiness was evident. I held onto him longer than I realized before he stepped back and asked me if things were okay. Tears were coming down my face and I hadn't mean to start crying but I was.

"Daddy, Daddy!" Anya called out still strapped inside of her car seat.

"I'm sorry darling," he responded unbuckling her.

Grabbing my purse, folders and attaché case; I looked at the two of them in awe as to how this man could come outta nowhere and just melt our hearts.

In his car I saw clothes, a few duffel bags and other personal items. I was about to question him when he turned and hugged us both saying;

"I'm here now just like you wanted me to be."

"Daddy you gonna be here in the morning when I wake up," Anya asked not realizing his intentions.

"Yeah Chico, daddy is gonna be here a lot of mornings when you wake up," he replied kissing us both.

"Wow, I'm almost afraid to ask what made you finally decide to do this."

"Why can't missing y'all be enough?"

Looking at him sideways, I knew there had to be more to it than that, but I just accepted what he was saying for right now. At the end of the day he was here and we were going to be a family.

DICKMITIZED

Publisher's Note: This is a work of fiction. Any resemblance to actual persons living or dead - references to real people, events, songs, business establishments or locales is purely coincidental. All characters are fictional, all events are imaginative.
QUEEN
Copyright © 2016 JUSTIN YOUNG
All rights reserved. This book for licensed for your personal enjoyment. This book or any portion thereof may not be reproduced or used in any manner whatsoever without the express written permission of the publisher except for the use of brief quotations in a book review. Send all requests to
accessjustinyoung@gmail.com

QUEEN

"I could get used to laying on you," she spoke just slightly above the music that was playing in the background. We were entwined in each other's arms, her head on my chest, my fingers in her hair and one of her legs lying across my own.

"I would hope so. This feels too good for it to only be something that's temporary."

A moment passed before she raised her head up and looked me in my eyes, then rested her head back in position. She smirked then snuggled a little tighter.

"Why you do that?" I questioned fingering the strands of hair close by her forehead

"Neither of us wants to create a situation. This works…for now."

'For now', her words lingered and this time, it was me that smirked and shook my head. I was in the dark so I knew she couldn't see my face, but I was in agreement. We didn't need to make things harder than what they were so even though she was candid, for the time being I knew she was right. I wasn't going to force something that I wasn't in a position to do something about in the event she called my bluff. We lived in two different cities and both of our careers were catapulting us to another level. She was a model and I was a photographer. It just so happened that we found ourselves in the same cities whenever we could. It was in these moments that we got glimpses of what our relationship would look like in the event we really were honest about where we could go together with this.

I may very well just be overthinking the process. I raised her chin up and bent down to kiss her lips. The fullness against mine only increased my desire to feel her more, greedily I kissed her mouth eagerly transferring the intensity between us both, sucking and pulling. She reached up to touch the side of my face while my thoughts ran on repeat: *these lips*. I had seen them in so many pictures before modeling, but nothing compared to feeling them in the flesh against my own. Everywhere our bodies connected, her skin against mine, her weight against me, and her soft touches only made my arousal fully swell. Her scent was heavenly, a subtle perfume that made you fight the temptation to inhale deeply, but forced you to do it anyway.

I pulled her closer to me and she shifted her weight straddling on top of me. The movement was swift as I cupped her ass in my hands and squeezed the softness while pressing my arousal against her sex. It was all about positioning and I was maneuvering myself to be permanent in her life. My fingertips roamed along her body seeking its own pleasure, its own satisfaction as every inch was caressed and massaged while we continued kissing on one another. In the background Trey Songz, *'Massage'* played:

"Do you miss me? 'cause I miss you, and the sexy lil thing you make your lips do, the way your hips move..."

Her hair fell down over my face as she bent down to caress it, but quickly she grabbed it and repositioned it to the other side of her head. Even in the dark I could sense her hunger, her impatience. I had awakened something deep within her being with our kisses as my own lustful passion ignited and began to take over. For a quick second I thought about the condom that rested on the nightstand, within arm's reach, even looked in its direction knowing that I needed to put it on for what was about to happen. Just as I considered sitting up, she pressed her lips back against mine forcing my mouth open. I wrapped my arms around her and closed my eyes, our tongues danced with one another as we no longer breathed separately, but as one.

Before I had realized it, she had reached within my waistband and held in her hand my throbbing cock. I didn't have to tell her to squeeze it because she immediately stroked and pulled on it before releasing it from out of my boxers and setting it against her sex where it pressed hard against her entrance. I felt the heat and was teased by her wetness and the stubble of her pubic hair, as the thin fabric of her thong allowed me semi entry. I needed to be inside of her, needed for her to feel my entire length, needed to lose myself in her. My thoughts raced, my blood raced faster, the only thing that moved slowly was our movements as we both were making sure the other was getting the attention that was required and needed after it had been so long since we had seen one another.

"Do you want me?" she stopped and whispered.

"More than you know right now." I leaned up and grabbed the back of her head forcing her mouth back onto mine.

Reaching back down, she rose up, grabbed my cock and slowly put it inside of her. One of my hands was already resting on her ass, so I took one finger and held her thong to the side as she took a little of me at a time. Her movements were subtle at first, easing in and out, fitting me inside. I watched in between her legs the silhouette of her sex as I entered and exited.

Did she realize what she had done? I thought, knowing that we weren't protected and any slip- ups could potentially force us to make a decision neither of us had ever spoken about. Yet, I was worried all of two seconds because this woman at this very moment made me feel like I could tell her that I love her. At this moment, all of those months of flirting back n' forth, texting, and sharing intimate conversations made me buy more into the fantasy that she really belonged to me. I wanted this to be more than one of our rendezvous. I wanted her to feel exactly in the way that I touched her that she had touched something within me too. I wanted each kiss to leave an imprint on her mind, not just how good my lips felt, but in the way that I kissed her back. I wanted something to click within her being that this was more than a weekend tryst.

Grabbing her hips, I encouraged her to make me feel how good her love felt, to be deep inside of her.

"You playing," I said in reaction to her only taking short dips. She leaned backward and began riding me the way I liked while I held her breast in my hands and played with her nipples. Every so often a moan would escape from her lips and I would try to do whatever I had done to make her moan again. I knew she was holding it in, refusing to be broken. I smiled, however, in my head because I knew she was enjoying it. I knew tomorrow that she would be somewhere miles away from me and these very moments would pop up and cause her to clench her legs. Without a doubt, I knew.

"Lay down," I suggested, preparing to take over. I knew that I wanted to taste her, the thought ran through my mind as she shifted the pillows on the bed spreading her legs to receive me. Erykah Badu's *In Love with You* began playing and I slowly leaned forward kissing her belly button moving up to her breast, up to her neck until I found the lips that I had fallen in love with initially.

I positioned myself on top and entered her slowly. The mood of the song dictated my pace as I wrapped my arms around this woman and held onto her tightly.

"You are so beautiful to me," I whispered in her ear.

The cool wetness on the side of my face made me pause for a second before I realized she had tears flowing down the side of her face. That was evidence to me that this meant more than what she had allowed herself to express. I kissed her tears away to show her that I was here, although scared just like she was to take the next step, but, I was willing.

"You okay?"

She shook her head yes.

"I'm here," I reassured.

"I know."

Moments later on the verge of climaxing, I waited until I couldn't hold back any longer before pulling out and spilling my seed on a nearby towel that hung at the foot of the bed. Exhausted I fell back on my side as she leaned back and snuggled against me. Feeling out of breath I tried to not sound as winded as I thought it appeared, but the temperature in the room had risen and it just wasn't enough fresh air circulating.

"I know you asked me was I okay, but are you?" she asked concerned.

Her question made me laugh because it made me feel slightly older than what I was. For the next few minutes, we laid in each other's arms talking about various projects that we had been booked for. The excitement was all in her voice as I listened and marveled at how she appreciated the smallest of gestures that were bestowed upon her to get her to where she was at right now. I knew that feeling because my own journey held a similar testimony of endurance and faith. It was oftentimes discouraging chasing after a dream that you only believed in, that you could only see, and that you wanted so badly to catch on.

"You know I just gotta stand by the idea that if I'm patient, consistent and faithful, I will definitely get to where I want to be."

"That's why I like opening up to you because you make me feel so safe and wanted," she admitted.

The night was early, I had caught my second wind and wasn't no telling when we were going to sleep, but I figured that could be done on the flight. Tonight, this woman wasn't the highly sought after model who appeared on the covers of several well-known male magazines, no, tonight she was my plain Jane. The next set of movements ignited a part two, where she requested several pillows to lay upon. Before I knew it though, she was singing another tune as this position allowed me to penetrate her a little deeper than what she expected. Although she was propped on top of several pillows, I had pushed one of her legs at the knee towards her stomach. The combination of what I felt between her legs and hearing her tell me I was touching a new spot only drove me to dig a little deeper and a little harder.

She pulled at the sheets, grabbing at everything and anything around while moaning loudly within the pillow. I wasn't stopping. Not until both of us wanted to tap out. This was erotic, all the elements of lovemaking and fucking. This time, when we collapsed our eyes didn't open back up again until later in the morning where we found ourselves rushing to get packed. Our flights were leaving around the same time so I packed everything up in one car, grabbed some fruit that was downstairs in the hotel then waited until she did her final walk through in the room to make sure she hadn't left anything.

"Why are you looking at me like that?"

"Because...you do something to me," I quickly responded. I wasn't for certain how I was looking at her, but I knew my thoughts were beyond the car that we were traveling in, wondering if this woman's soul could be equally yoked to mine. Could this moment that we were in last beyond days, weeks and months? Was it worth trying or would our agendas complicate things? I thought about all of this while staring at profile the profile of her beautiful face.

"See? You're being weird right now." She turned to look at me, taking her eyes off of the road. Our eyes lingered on each other for a second before she turned and smiled, her cheeks rising.

I laughed sensing that I was making her blush. It was funny to see how radiant yet fleeting it was. A car flashed passed us obviously late for whatever their final destination was supposed to be.

"That shit is crazy how people be driving and don't be getting nowhere but a few cars up."

On my shirt hung a piece of lint that I picked at before reaching to grab the knob on the radio. It was something about this particular song that touched me, although I didn't know the lyrics. It was soulful, had depth and meaning, spoke about love and all of its potential. For a second, I closed my eyes, losing myself in its melodic rhythm, every so often moving my head to the beat. She sang the words along with the artist. Her voice was killing the song, but I liked her boldness as well as showing vulnerability.

The car violently jerking to the side forced me to open my eyes and only in time to see us heading towards the wall. I remembered throwing my hands up before the sound of the impact forced me into a state of darkness. When I opened my eyes, it took some adjusting before I realized that I was in the hospital and what had happened. My mouth was dry and my body still ached. On the other side of the curtain, I could sense someone there by the whimpering noises I heard. I couldn't speak as clearly as I thought, but I still tried getting the nurse's attention to inquire about what happened.

"Hello, sir. How are you feeling this morning?" the nurse asked.

Pointing to my throat I tried insisting that I needed a drink and she accommodated. Propping the bed up by remote, I sat up still in disbelief to what had happened. The curtain in the room that separated both sides only allowed me to visually see the bottom half of a set of legs. As the nurse continued to run off her checklist of things, my curiosity of who was beyond the curtain only piqued. The quiet sobs that were being released felt like I knew and was connected to them.

Could it be her? I wondered. The pain in my head made me close my eyes and inhale deeply.

"It looks like you're in a little pain, sir. Give me a second and I'll make things a little more comfortable."

I shook my head okay and watched as the nurse went into her pocket to pull out a syringe, walked to the IV and transferred the contents. The pain forced me to close my eyes and slowly I slipped back into the darkness.

The next time I felt aware of my surroundings was first by touch, the warmth of someone holding my hand and then the weight of something on my thigh. Though I didn't hear it at first, the sound of music softly playing caused me to open my eyes. There she was laying her head on me turned in the opposite direction. Reaching over, I touched the crown of her head stroking the length of her long hair. Even in this room right now there was no other place I would rather be than to be with her.

"Hey you."

In slow motion, it seemed, she raised her head to turn to me. Our eyes connected and all I could say was, "Baby."

The tears began to fall from her eyes as I looked at the side of her face where she now had a bandaged covering almost half. The long hair that once fell to her shoulders now was shaved on one side. I reached out to touch her, but she turned slightly away, seemingly embarrassed or ashamed, I didn't know.

Her career, I thought immediately.

Her tears began falling more rapidly which made mine begin to swell in my eyes.

"Come here," I requested pulling her into the bed with me comforting her while rubbing her back. It was like a floodgate opening as her body shook with deep sobs and weeping. I knew what this potentially meant for her, which saddened me more knowing what her dreams and aspirations meant.

"We will get through this, I promise."

"You can't say that," she replied. "Look at me! I should've never come to Virginia."

I let her vent, allowed her to be angry and get her frustrations out. Her tears slowly dried up, replaced now with anger and regret. She rose up from the bed prepared to get out until I reached for her wrist.

"I love you, we will get through this." The words fell out of my mouth with conviction.

It stopped her for a second where she looked down and measured me with her eyes. I pulled her back towards the bed where my own pain was creeping back and assured her, "You have always been beautiful to me. This doesn't change that or the way I feel about you. I love you and I am promising you that we will get through this together."

Whatever it took, I knew nothing was by chance. It was a blessing to be alive because things could've turned out differently. Previously when I had questioned myself if she was my one, I knew that this situation was confirmation because I felt closer to her now than ever before.

"Do you know what you are saying?" she asked.

"I do, Queen. You ignited something within me before the accident that scared me because I didn't know how real it was. It seemed too cliché, but I know I don't want to lose you. There is no going back to normal. This is what it's supposed to be."

In our careers, there were chances and challenges that we maneuvered to get to where we ultimately wanted to be. In love, however, the maneuvering wasn't as forgiving, but there comes a time when you have to throw two sheets to the wind and just jump. Looking into her eyes, I was prepared to do just that.

I was ready…we could fall but I knew we would soar!

CHOOSE EITHER WINE GLASSES OR CANVASES

MATERIALS SUPPLIED

FOR MORE INFO EMAIL:
ACCESSJUSTINYOUNG@GMAIL.COM

Interested in participating in or putting together a Paint n' Sip with your friends… contact me to host/instruct.
Group rates available.

DICKMITIZED

Follow the author on these social media sites:
FACEBOOK: JUSTIN Q YOUNG
TWITTER: OFFICIALAUTHORQ
INSTAGRAM: firstborn_design
PINTEREST: JQYOUNG76

ACCESSJUSTINYOUNG@GMAIL.COM
ITEMS CAN BE PURCHASED AT THE FOLLOWING AS
WELL AS SHIPPED TO PRISONS.

Make money orders payable to Justin Young,
P.O. Box 2594, Glen Allen, Va 23058

JUSTIN "Q" YOUNG

THANK YOU FOR THE SUPPORT!